JOHN, Laurie

Jessica turned her head just enough to see that there was no sign of sympathy in the officers' faces. Each one had a gun trained on the twins. At the sight of the guns, Jessica sprang into action. "Into the Jeep!" she whispered wildly, pushing Elizabeth in front of her. She grabbed the door handle and shoved her sister inside. Then she raced to the driver's door and dove in herself, as one of the police officers opened fire. Jessica squeezed the Jeep out of the parking space and careened down the street. In the rearview mirror, she saw the officers running to their patrol car.

"Stop, Jessica," Elizabeth stammered. "Oh, my God. I can't believe we're running from the police."

"They'll never believe us!" Jessica wailed. "I'm on the videotape, not Scott. Don't you see, Liz? Don't you get it? We're wanted for murder, Elizabeth! We've got to escape!"

Bantam Books in the Sweet Valley University series:

SWEET VALLEY UNIVERSITY™

THRILLER EDITION

Wanted for Murder

Written by
Laurie John

Created by
FRANCINE PASCAL

BANTAM BOOKS
NEW YORK · TORONTO · LONDON · SYDNEY · AUCKLAND

WANTED FOR MURDER
A BANTAM BOOK 0 553 40988 3

Originally published in USA by Bantam Books

First publication in Great Britain

PRINTING HISTORY
Bantam edition published 1995

Conceived by Francine Pascal

Produced by Daniel Weiss Associates, Inc,
33 West 17th Street, New York, NY 10011

Bantam Books are published by Transworld Publishers Ltd,
61–63 Uxbridge Road, Ealing, London W5 5SA,
in Australia by Transworld Publishers (Australia) Pty Ltd,
15–25 Helles Avenue, Moorebank, NSW 2170,
and in New Zealand by Transworld Publishers (NZ) Ltd,
3 William Pickering Drive, Albany, Auckland.

Printed and bound in Great Britain by
Cox & Wyman Ltd, Reading, Berkshire.

To William Benjamin Rubin

Chapter
One

Jessica Wakefield bounded out the front door of her family's home in Sweet Valley, California. "I just talked to Steven," she announced to her identical twin sister. "And I couldn't change his mind—he's really giving up a ski trip in order to lie around his apartment all week. And to think that I always considered *you* the most boring person in the family."

At the moment, Jessica thought, her sister looked anything but bored. Elizabeth stood gazing into the dark eyes of her boyfriend—tall, broad-shouldered Tom Watts.

Elizabeth and Tom had started dating during the twins' first semester of college at Sweet Valley University. The two worked together at the campus television station and had spent practically all their time together since school started. Now, with visible reluctance, Elizabeth wrenched her attention away from Tom's chiseled features.

"Have some sympathy, Jess," she said. "It's not as though Steven *wants* to miss the trip."

Jessica tossed her backpack into the already full backseat of their Jeep. "Then he should come with us."

"He sounded pretty sick when we talked to him last night—"

"He sounds even worse this morning," Jessica interrupted cheerfully. "But it's not like he has malaria or anything—it's just the flu. I really thought he'd change his mind."

"Well, I'm not surprised," Elizabeth said. "Steven's too sensible to go skiing when he's so sick."

"He'd feel three hundred times better if he came to Vail—just getting out of this heat would make him happier."

Tom shook his head. "I doubt it. I wish Steven and Billie could be there, too. But two full days of driving would be murder in his condition."

"I guess," Jessica said with a shrug. "Especially in this weather! I don't remember it ever being this hot in December." She opened the driver's door of the Jeep and fanned the ovenlike interior with her arms.

Tom nodded. "And according to the weather reports, the heat wave covers most of California and southern Nevada—that's your whole first day of driving. Poor Steven would die before you made it."

"To tell you the truth," Elizabeth said, "I feel kind of guilty about running off to Vail while he's stuck at home feeling so rotten."

Jessica dismissed Steven's plight with a wave of her hand. "Aw, he doesn't have it so rough. Billie will wait on him hand and foot for the next week."

"You're probably right," Elizabeth said. "I bet she'll spend the whole week making him tea and taking his temperature. I hate to say it, but Steven can be a real baby when he's sick."

"All men are babies when they're sick," Jessica corrected her. Tom opened his mouth to protest, but Jessica cut him off. "Billie's the one I feel sorry for. She's missing out on the ski trip of the century just because her boyfriend's got a little sniffle. What a crummy way to spend the last week of winter break!"

"We'll bring them a souvenir," Elizabeth said.

Jessica narrowed her eyes. "The worst part is that I was counting on Steven to lend me some extra bucks for this trip."

Tom put his hand on his heart. "Your sympathy for your brother is touching, Jessica."

"I'd feel better if Mom and Dad hadn't left on that business trip this morning," Elizabeth said. Jessica rolled her eyes. Elizabeth was never happy unless she was playing mother hen to somebody. "At least if they were in town, somebody would be nearby to check in on Steven now and then."

"Palm Springs!" Jessica scoffed. "Some business trip!"

"So Mom has a glamorous profession—give them a break! Why are you on *their* case now?"

"I'm not," Jessica said with a dramatic sigh. "But you'd think they could have given us a *little* extra money for Vail."

"Grandma and Grandpa gave us each five hundred dollars for Christmas," Elizabeth pointed out. "And I've still got a little left from my allowance for first semester. We'll manage."

"We'd do more than *manage* if we had money from Mom and Dad, too. They're still mad because I had that minor cash-flow problem last semester."

Elizabeth turned on her with the amused look that always infuriated Jessica. "*Minor* cash-flow problem? Jessica, they gave you enough money to last until Christmas and you ran through it before first semester was halfway over!"

"So? I had expenses. Like you would know anything about it, Liz. You have no life."

Elizabeth's eyes twinkled in the bright morning sunlight. To Jessica's annoyance, she still looked amused. "After spending the first week of winter break trying to hide *your* life last semester from Mom and Dad, I'm pretty happy that I don't have a life of my own—by your standards."

Jessica grimaced. "I'm surprised we were able to keep it from them as long as we did."

"After last week, not to mention last semester, I think we both deserve this trip."

"What about money, Liz?" Tom asked, concerned. "Will you have enough?"

"It'll be a little tight," Elizabeth admitted, "but we'll be fine. We should have just enough for gas, food, lift tickets, and our room at the resort."

"What about emergencies?" Tom asked, his deep voice growing more intense. "You've got more than a thousand miles to go each way. What if the Jeep breaks down when you're out in the middle of the desert somewhere? What if—"

Elizabeth smiled. "Don't worry! We'll be all right."

Tom frowned, his eyes full of concern. "I'm not sure it's a good idea for you to drive all that way by yourself."

"She's not by herself," Jessica reminded him acidly. "She's with me."

Elizabeth placed a hand on Tom's arm. "We're not children, Tom. We're eighteen years old!"

Jessica grinned. "Together, we're thirty-six!"

"I know, but I felt better about you driving when I thought you'd be in a caravan with Steven and Billie."

Jessica tossed her long blond hair over her shoulder. "I, for one, don't need my big brother to look out for me."

Tom raised his eyebrows. "Oh, really?" he asked.

5

"Don't you dare bring up last semester!" Jessica warned him.

"I won't," Tom said. "But you two would be a lot safer with a guy in the car. Maybe I should cash in my plane tickets and ride with you, instead of meeting you in Vail. Danny and Isabella won't mind if I don't fly to Colorado with them."

"I'll mind!" Elizabeth said. "You know, Tom, Jessica and I got along just fine for eighteen years without you to keep an eye on us. I think we can manage for two days."

"Besides," Jessica pointed out, "you'll lose a ton of money if you cancel your plane reservations this late."

"Then maybe you two should reconsider and fly into Denver tomorrow with us."

"Right," Jessica said with a snort. "And we'll use our good looks to pay for the airline tickets."

Tom took Elizabeth's face gently into his hands and stared into her blue-green eyes. "In that case, you've got enough currency here to charter the Concorde."

Jessica rolled her own blue-green eyes. "Oh, please."

Elizabeth placed a hand on her boyfriend's arm. "Tom, you know we can't afford to fly."

"Fly?" Jessica asked. "I couldn't even afford any new ski suits! There's nothing like looking good on the slopes to catch the attention of cute skiers."

6

"You've never needed any help picking up guys," Elizabeth reminded her.

"You have a point there," Jessica admitted, bending to admire her tanned face in the side-view mirror. She adjusted the straps on her skin-baring white top. "I'll be gorgeous no matter what I'm wearing." With their wholesome good looks and size-six figures, both of the Wakefield twins were used to attracting attention from the opposite sex. And Jessica, at least, relished that kind of attention.

"My offer still stands, Elizabeth," Tom said seriously. "I'll lend you the money for the airfare—Jessica's too. You pay me back whenever you can."

Elizabeth shook her head. "No way. You can't afford it. Besides, Jessica and I are looking forward to this road trip." She smiled warmly at her sister. "Last semester was so busy that we've hardly seen each other in months. The drive will give us time to talk for a change."

Tom frowned. "I know I'm being silly. But I have this totally irrational feeling that you're heading for trouble."

"Then we're perfectly safe," Jessica said, slamming the driver's-side door. "Because at this rate, we'll never even leave Sweet Valley! Come on, Liz," she called through the open window. "You were the one who wanted to be on the road by nine o'clock."

Elizabeth laughed. "All right, all right. Just

give us a chance to say good-bye." She stood on her toes to kiss Tom.

"You've been saying good-bye for the last two days!" Jessica exclaimed.

Tom wrapped his arms around Elizabeth and lifted her off the ground as they kissed.

Jessica rolled her eyes. "Have you guys heard one word that I've said? Elizabeth? It's time to go!"

"I hear you," Elizabeth said absentmindedly as her sneakers made contact with the driveway. Her eyes hadn't moved from Tom's handsome face. "But parting is such sweet sorrow."

Jessica groaned. "How can someone who looks so much like me be such a geek?"

"I still don't know about letting you drive all that way by yourselves," Tom began again.

Jessica's mouth dropped open. "Letting us? I didn't know we needed your permission."

"Stop being so overprotective, Tom!" Elizabeth said, an edge of annoyance creeping into her voice. "We're driving to Vail by ourselves. And that's that!"

Tom nodded. "Okay. I'm sorry I'm being a jerk. But promise you'll call me when you stop for the night. I'll be in my dorm room."

"Aren't the dorms closed for break?" Jessica asked.

Tom shrugged. "I got special permission to stay during break. I said I was needed at the television station. Power of the press, you know."

"Oh," Jessica said, yawning.

"Well, I'll call you later if it will make you feel better," Elizabeth said. "But nothing is going to go wrong."

"Where are you planning to stop tonight?"

"We'll have about ten hours of driving time today." Elizabeth threw Jessica a knowing glance. "Nine, with Jess at the wheel. Either way, we're through California and Nevada, across a little corner of Arizona, and into Utah before dark. We'll get a motel room there."

"So I should hear from you around seven."

Elizabeth nodded. "And you'll see me in Vail tomorrow night, so stop worrying. We'll be just in time to celebrate New Year's Eve with you, Danny, and Isabella."

"And the cutest male skier in Colorado," Jessica added. "As soon as I decide who he is and make him fall madly in love with me."

Jessica was happy that her glamorous friend Isabella Ricci had begun dating Danny Wyatt, Tom's roommate at SVU. But with everyone else paired off on this trip, she felt dangerously close to being a fifth wheel. She was certain she could find a handsome, unattached skier—but not until she could get her sister away from her own good-looking, attached student reporter.

"Come on, Liz," she urged. "I can't say hello to my skier until you finish saying good-bye to

9

him. We want to get to Vail in time for New Year's Eve—not Groundhog Day."

Tom wrapped his arms around Elizabeth's slender figure and pulled her to him for another kiss. "Promise me you'll be careful," he said.

Elizabeth sighed. "This is starting to get irritating."

"It certainly is," Jessica piped up. "And everybody accuses *me* of never being on time! Come on, let's get this road trip on the road!"

Elizabeth climbed into the Jeep and then leaned out the window for one last kiss. "Don't worry, Tom. We're going to have a nice, quiet, boring drive."

Tom sighed. "I hope so," he said.

"*I* don't," Jessica muttered. Then she gunned the engine and switched on the radio, loud.

The roof of the old sedan gave shade from the sun blazing in the white-hot Nevada sky. But even the shade gave no relief from the heat. Winters in southern Nevada tended to be mild, but this had been the warmest December anyone could remember. The radio announcer's crackling voice gave the current temperature as eighty-five degrees, though it was only eleven o'clock in the morning. The glaring sunlight—and the fact that it was, after all, December 30—made the day seem hotter. And it was a dry, penetrating heat that scorched the earth and set people's nerves on edge.

The young man in the beat-up Oldsmobile had trained himself to keep his cool in any temperature. Just the same, he decided, things were beginning to heat up in Nevada in more ways than one. It was time to get out of this state. Utah was no good—he'd already been there. He'd have to cross the border soon, probably into California. But for now, he had a job to do.

He parked the car on the side of the dusty road, just past a gas station. Then he peered through the cracked windshield, his sharp eyes squinting from beneath the brim of his Stetson as he scanned the scene. The desert stretched around him—low, dried-out hills in shades of tan and gold, dotted with sagebrush. The service station was the only building in sight. In the distance behind it, Tonovah Summit rose from the desert to a height of six thousand feet.

He took note of the single, old-fashioned gas pump, the dirt-stained windows, and the faded sign that announced GAS! OIL! CHERRY COLA! He nodded thoughtfully. "Just right," he drawled to his reflection in the scratched side-view mirror. A mom-and-pop kind of place smack in the middle of the desert. Inside, just two clerks playing cards behind the register. A good, fast secondary road without much traffic.

He grinned, swept off the Stetson, and smoothed his hair. Then he aimed his finger as if it were a gun. "It's show time."

The young man knotted a faded blue bandanna around his neck, cowboy style, and raised it to cover his mouth and nose. He selected a gun—a Colt .45 revolver—from the three in his canvas duffel bag. The Colt was his favorite gun—the only gun he felt any real ownership for. The others were a constantly changing round of pawn-shop finds, intended to throw the police off the track. It wouldn't do to commit every crime with the same gun. That would establish too much of a pattern. But he couldn't bring himself to give up his Colt. He loaded the revolver with a spin of the cylinder. Then he leaped from the car.

A minute later he threw open the door of the gas station and pointed the revolver at the white-haired man and the tall, gaunt woman behind the counter. The cards they'd been playing with cascaded to the floor.

"This is what you call a stickup," the young man said in a friendly, conversational tone. "Here's the way it works. You both do just like I say, and nobody gets hurt. Mister, you grab me one of those cherry colas while this charming creature—your wife?"

Both the man and woman nodded slightly, their eyes still riveted to the pistol.

The young man smiled. "Your wife here opens up that cash register and pulls out all the bills inside," he continued. "Then you put the cash and the cola in one of them paper bags for me, and I'll be on my way. And everybody stays healthy." He kept his voice light, but his gray eyes were as cold as steel. "Now how does that sound to you?"

The old man's hands were shaking as he reached into the cooler behind him for the cherry cola. The young man felt the same rush of power that holdups always gave him. He stepped forward and poked the gun against the woman's temple. She screamed.

He glared at her. "I asked you a question!"

"It sounds fine," the old man blurted, almost dropping the bottle of soda. "Cora, just do like he says."

The woman opened the cash register drawer with a loud *ding* and started fumbling with the bills inside. "Mister, we don't want any trouble," she said, almost in a whisper. "You can have everything we've got." A paper bag rattled as she shoved a thick wad of cash inside with trembling hands.

The young man flashed a grin. "Now I'll be moseying on out of here. Pleasure doing business with you folks." He sauntered to the door, but then wheeled around to face the couple.

A shot rang out. The old man staggered as if he'd been hit. But it was the telephone on the wall behind him that shattered, raining bits of metal and plastic on the floor. The young man laughed. That little trick was always good for another scare. He loved the look of terror in the woman's eyes.

He winked at her over the blue bandanna. Then he ambled to the door of the gas station, careful to appear nonchalant. He listened for the slow exhalations of breath behind him that meant his victims were feeling relieved. Then he whirled on the heel of his boot and popped off two quick but expertly aimed shots. For an instant, the woman screamed as her husband staggered and fell. Then her voice was cut short.

In the silence, the wooden screen door banged like another gunshot as the young man stepped outside into the sun's glare. Without glancing back, he sprinted to the sedan. Then he sped off, heading west, as heat waves shimmered like water on the highway ahead.

Elizabeth slid into the driver's seat as Jessica emerged from a roadside convenience store carrying a paper bag and a can of soda.

"What took you so long?" Elizabeth asked. "I thought you were just getting some cookies. What did you do—hold up the place?"

"Yeah!" Jessica said gleefully. "This is a stickup!" She blew through her drinking straw, shooting the paper wrapper into Elizabeth's face. "Actually," she explained, "I would have been out a lot sooner. But the clerk was about twenty-six years old, with curly black hair and biceps to die for."

Elizabeth shook her head and steered the Jeep

out of the parking lot. "That seems perfectly logical to you, doesn't it?"

"Logic? That's a nasty thing to bring up while we're on vacation."

Elizabeth grinned. "Sorry. All I mean is that whenever you see a good-looking guy, flirting with him just naturally takes precedence over everything else."

"Well, yes," Jessica said, gesturing with a chocolate-chip cookie. "What's your point?"

Elizabeth couldn't help laughing. "You're one of a kind!"

"That means a lot, coming from my mirror image."

"Well, mirror image, I don't want to stop again until we're in Nevada—no matter how many cute guys there are. We don't need gas, and you can't possibly need any more root beer. That must be your tenth one today."

Jessica gave her an injured look. "We're in the Mojave Desert, Liz. We've got a whole hour of desert driving before we get to Baker—maybe longer, since you drive like somebody's great-grandfather. You're supposed to bring plenty of liquids when driving through the desert."

Elizabeth shook her head. "This is a little stretch of the Mojave; it's not the Sahara," she said, amused.

"The temperature can hit more than a hundred

and thirty degrees in Death Valley! I read that somewhere."

"That's in the summer, Jess, and we're not driving through Death Valley." Elizabeth grinned. "I'm surprised you even know what state we're in, you're so clueless about geography."

"Well, when the Jeep breaks down a thousand miles away from civilization and we're crawling over sand dunes in the middle of the desert, I'll be happy to have an extra root beer—and you'll just have to be thirsty."

Elizabeth laughed. "In that case, you could have at least picked me up a diet soda, as long as you were in there."

Jessica reached into the paper bag. "I thought you'd never ask. One diet soda, coming up. I got you an apple, too—just in case you're still paranoid about gaining weight."

"I am not paranoid!" Elizabeth protested. "It's just that every chocolate-chip cookie in that box is conspiring against my hips. I thought I was going to college to gain knowledge and culture—not two dress sizes! Now that we're mirror images again, I'd like to stay that way."

"Don't worry. You're almost as beautiful as me."

"You know, Jess, I'm really happy we're taking this road trip. First semester was so weird; you and I were so wrapped up in our own problems that

16

we hardly even saw each other. I'm glad we're rooming together again."

Jessica took a long sip of her root beer. "Me too!" she declared. "But I don't want to think about school. We're about to have the greatest ski vacation in the history of the Rocky Mountains. This is no time to talk about SVU—let's see what the folks in Barstow listen to on the radio." Snatches of voices, music, and static spurted out in quick succession as she twirled the radio dial.

Jessica made a face. "Nothing but oldies. Oh, well!" She shrugged and began singing along to "The Way You Do the Things You Do" in a tuneless but enthusiastic voice. "Come on, Liz! Sing!"

Years earlier, Elizabeth had resigned herself to the fact that nobody in the Wakefield family had a shred of singing ability. But now she laughed and joined in, just as loudly and as happily as her sister.

Special Agent Jeff Marks looked up from his computer screen and rubbed his eyes. For two hours, he'd been searching Department of Motor Vehicles records on his computer at the FBI's office in Nevada—to no avail. As lead agent at the Carson City field office, he had all the resources of the Bureau and the police departments of two states at his disposal. But he still didn't have enough information on the car owner he desperately wanted to find. The car owner who had robbed a string of stores and gas stations across

Utah and Nevada—if Jeff's theory was correct. If the fatal robberies over the last three weeks really were connected.

Once again, Jeff checked the police report from the latest armed robbery. It had occurred the day before, at a tiny convenience store in central Nevada. About three hundred dollars seemed to be missing; nobody ever kept close track of the cash at those little roadside stops. The lone clerk had to be airlifted to the hospital in Reno, with a nasty head wound. She'd been hit with a heavy object—maybe a pistol. So far, the clerk was still alive, but she hadn't regained consciousness. Jeff knew she might never wake up to answer any questions. As usual, the store had no surveillance cameras, so there was no description of the perpetrator. Jeff sighed. It was becoming a familiar story.

A passing motorist had remembered seeing a blue or gray sedan in front of the store sometime in the afternoon, within an hour or two of the incident. No make. No model. No year.

"Heck, I don't even know if that car is connected to the robbery," Jeff said aloud. "Or if it's the same blue sedan that was at the Stillwater crime scene, or the gray car spotted at the holdup near Salt Lake. A lot of people drive blue or gray sedans. My *grandmother* drives a blue sedan!"

He swigged a mouthful of lukewarm coffee and ran a hand through his thick brown hair.

Great, I'm talking to myself now. And even that was getting him nowhere. At this point, the car was the only breakthrough, and it was precious little. It was the only tangible evidence—if you could call a few sketchy descriptions evidence—that the robberies had been committed by the same person.

Jeff had been an FBI agent long enough to know when to trust his instincts. And every fiber in his body was telling him—screaming to him—that the person who hit the store near Eureka was the same one who'd held up the deserted diner in Stillwater, Nevada, on a rainy, gut-wrenching night ten days earlier.

Jeff felt his eyes moistening as he stared at the framed photograph that sat on his desk. Summer O'Brian. The face that smiled back at him had the ebony hair and high cheekbones of her mother's Shoshone Indian heritage combined with her Irish father's lighter skin and sparkling blue-green eyes.

"I'll find the person who did this," he whispered to the woman in the photograph. "I swear I will."

A sound like gunshots rang through the air, and Jeff jumped. But it was only a rapping on his door. Special Agent Keisha Williamson poked her head into his office. "Jeff, there's been another armed robbery," she said, glancing at a police report in her hand. "At a service station in the desert, a little north of Tonovah. An elderly couple is dead."

"Witnesses?"

She shook her head and handed him the report. "None. The local sheriff's department is treating it as a separate incident, unrelated to any of the others. They may be right. But I thought you'd want to know about it."

"Any reports of a blue or gray sedan?"

"No reports of anything."

"The reports from the Wendover case say that a passerby noticed a young man with light-brown hair in the store's parking lot that evening. Were there any reports like that?"

Keisha shook her head. "Jeff, I told you there were no witnesses. Besides, you know that report from Wendover is meaningless. The witness couldn't provide any further description of the man, and she could only place him there within two hours of the robbery. It's not much of a lead."

Jeff sighed. "I know. But when you've got as little as we have to go on . . ." He paused, staring at Summer's photograph. Then he shook his head and looked back up at Keisha, whose dark eyes were full of sympathy. "What about a weapon, in the Tonovah case?"

"It was a Colt .45."

Jeff snapped his fingers. "That's it! A Colt was the murder weapon at the Stillwater diner."

Keisha shrugged. "True. But that's only one other incident. A lot of people have Colts. Maybe the local police are right, and they're not related."

Jeff shook his head. "They're related, all right," he said grimly.

"Well, the Colt still isn't much of a lead, Jeff. The other case reports mention a wide variety of weapons." She picked up a clipboard from Jeff's desk. "The Eureka clerk suffered head wounds from a blunt object. And the Salt Lake City robbery involved a Saturday night special, and the one outside of Wendover—"

"I know, I know. We've got almost as many different weapons as we have victims."

"That would seem to support the local authorities' theories about the robberies being unrelated," Keisha said carefully.

Jeff was already on his feet, strapping on his nine-millimeter semiautomatic pistol. "I'll take my gut feeling over their theories any day." He brushed past Keisha on his way out the door. Then he turned back into his office to gently lift the photograph of Summer O'Brian from his desk.

Jeff sprinted to the parking lot and jumped into his classic Mustang. Then he barreled south down the state highway out of Carson City, faster than a speeding bullet from a Colt .45.

Chapter Two

"Piece of junk!" Scott Culver yelled, kicking the wheel of the beat-up Oldsmobile. At one time, he guessed, the car had been blue. But now it was so faded and scratched that it was almost as colorless as the dull afternoon sky that glared overhead.

He raised the hood of the car and quickly found the problem. "The radiator's shot," he muttered, pulling back from the steam. He thought about walking to the nearest town, but that could be miles away—he didn't remember how close the next town was. And he didn't have a California map with him. Nevada, Arizona, and Utah he knew like he knew every crack and scuff in his old leather cowboy boots. But California was less familiar territory.

Unfortunately, California seemed as unbearably hot as Nevada had been. *It's no use trying to walk to civilization in this heat,* he decided. *At least, not until after sundown. Hopefully somebody will come by before then.*

Scott pulled his sweat-stained T-shirt over his head and threw it on the backseat of the car. Then he grabbed his Stetson from the front seat and placed it carefully on his head. The hat made his scalp sweat. But it was the only shade to be had in the middle of the desert. He was sure the temperature was above a hundred degrees inside the car. His best bet was to stay outside and hope that a passing motorist would give him a lift. But that could take hours; traffic was pretty sparse.

At least he was on the interstate, Scott reflected. If he had broken down on one of those minor, little-traveled trails through the desert, it could be days before another car passed.

He thought about hitchhiking, and wondered if he could find a bus anywhere. He sighed. "I can't do anything, as long as I'm stuck in the middle of the Mojave Desert with a broken-down radiator," he said aloud.

After a few minutes, a shimmer on the eastern horizon caught his eye. It was a car, and it was heading toward him. Scott crossed his fingers and waited. Finally the station wagon zoomed by, stirring up an eddy of hot air. The driver didn't even turn around.

Scott leaned morosely against the door of

24

the Oldsmobile. He kicked his boot-clad toe in the sand and tried to remember what New Year's weekend had looked like the year before—up north, in Montana. A foot of snow. Icicles hanging from the trees. Scott sighed again. It was no use, dreaming of cool weather. He could be waiting here for hours under the hot desert sky.

"Stop, in the name of love," Elizabeth sang along with the radio, "before you break my heart."

"Think it oh-oh-over," Jessica chimed in, wondering if her own voice was as off key as her sister's.

Elizabeth was still at the wheel—and driving much too slowly, in Jessica's opinion. Elizabeth kept remarking about how interesting the desert scenery was. Jessica just found it boring. Nothing but tan-colored dirt and short, scrubby plants.

And it was hot. True, she reminded herself, eighty-five degrees wasn't exactly unbearable. But eighty-five degrees in December felt a lot more blistering than eighty-five ever felt in July. Luckily, the Jeep had air-conditioning. Jessica felt sorry for anybody who was driving around without it today.

Come to think of it, she realized, hardly anyone seemed to be driving around at all today. She hadn't seen another car in ten minutes, not since an ugly old station wagon had zoomed past them like a rocket. *Unless you count that broken-down sedan up there. The one with the cowboy guy leaning against the door—the guy with no shirt on—*

"Stop!" she yelled suddenly.

"No, Jess," Elizabeth replied. "I'm doing the 'stop's. You're supposed to do the 'Think it oh-oh-over's."

"I mean stop the Jeep! It's an emergency!"

"I thought you used the bathroom at that gas station."

"Not that kind of emergency! Didn't you see that guy in the cowboy hat?"

Elizabeth glanced into the rearview mirror. "No, I hadn't really noticed. I guess his car broke down . . . but I don't think he's hurt or anything. He looks okay to me."

"*Okay?* He looks *okay?* Are you blind, Liz? Turn the Jeep around! That's the best-looking guy I've seen in months."

Elizabeth gave her one of those big-sisterly Jessica-is-at-it-again amused glances.

"Elizabeth! His car broke down. He's in trouble. You're the one who's always saying how important it is to help people in trouble. Besides, if we give him a lift to the next town, he'll be eternally grateful to me. You wouldn't want to screw up my first chance to date a real cowboy, would you?"

Elizabeth didn't even slow down. "Wearing a cowboy hat doesn't make someone a real cowboy, Jess," she said in a reasonable voice. "Everybody wears a cowboy hat in this part of the country."

"But Liz—"

"And he'll just have to be eternally grateful to an anonymous good Samaritan. We'll stop at the next gas station and send back a tow truck for him."

"Are you crazy? Did you see his body? He was incredibly gorgeous *and* he's wearing tight jeans and no shirt. Seriously, Liz, I'm in love."

"I thought you were saving yourself for the world's best-looking skier."

"Skiers wear too many clothes—I like cowboys better. Come on, Liz. You could make a U-turn right here and go back for him. Please?"

"Absolutely not, Jessica. No sensible person would pick up a complete stranger in the middle of nowhere."

"We're on vacation, Liz—this is no time to be sensible. You're being paranoid again. He's just a guy having car trouble. It's not as if he's some kind of outlaw."

Scott suddenly felt like a character in a beer commercial. Here he was, standing by his broken-down car with the California desert stretching around him, when a Jeep appeared in the west, like a mirage on the dusty interstate. Inside were two of the most beautiful blondes he'd ever seen. And the one in the passenger seat seemed to be staring right at him, with longing in her eyes.

Or maybe he was in a gum commercial. He could have sworn that the two girls were absolutely identical.

Scott rubbed his eyes after they'd passed. No, it wasn't a hallucination, he decided, watching the black Jeep grow smaller as it sped toward the horizon. Two gorgeous blondes had just flown by in a Jeep with California license plates, looking like angels.

He would have given anything if they had stopped.

"Jess, we've been sitting here for almost an hour," Elizabeth said, gesturing around the brightly lit roadside diner. "Plus, we took the time to send a tow truck back for that guy. We really ought to get back on the road."

The girls were sitting in a vinyl-covered booth in the small, air-conditioned diner. And although Elizabeth was protesting the amount of time they'd wasted there, Jessica could tell that her twin really didn't feel like moving any more than she did.

Jessica sipped her root beer until the straw made a slurping sound against the bottom of the glass. "I know," she said. "But we've been driving all day. I'm so sick of sitting in the car."

Elizabeth nodded. "Me too." She spread a map on the table between them. "Still, we haven't even crossed the Nevada border, see? We should be past Las Vegas by this hour. Now it'll be dark before we get to Utah for the night."

"Admit it, Liz—you're as tired as I am. It must be five o'clock or so, right? Why don't we order dinner, instead of just drinking soda? That gives us a legitimate reason for staying a while longer. I mean, we have to eat sometime, don't we?"

Elizabeth shrugged. "Okay, you go ahead. But I'm really not that hungry."

"Me neither. How about a piece of pie?"

"Jessica!"

"One little piece of pie won't make you gain weight."

Elizabeth smiled. "All right, you've convinced me!"

Jessica ordered two slices of pie from a dark-haired waitress on impossibly high heels. Then she pretended she was listening while Elizabeth traced their route on the map.

"Actually, it's not the end of the world if we don't make it to Utah tonight," Elizabeth pointed out. "Say we only get a little past Vegas and then decide to stop for the night. We can still make Vail the next evening—if we get up

29

extra early and put in a full day of driving."

Jessica didn't care whether they made it to Utah that night—or even what road they took, as long as cute skiers were at the end of it. But Elizabeth was always fascinated by that kind of trivia. Now she was using a lot of words like *gas mileage* and *interstate driving*. Jessica tuned out her sister's voice and waited for her apple pie, remembering to insert knowing nods at appropriate points.

Suddenly her attention was riveted to the doorway. She gasped.

Elizabeth looked up from the map. "What is it?"

"He's here!" Jessica hissed. "The cowboy with the broken-down car. He just walked in! Don't turn around. Do you think he sees us?"

The cowboy whisked off his hat and stood holding it in his hands as he scanned the interior of the diner. Jessica appraised him carefully. He was about twenty-three or twenty-four, she decided. He wasn't terribly tall; only a couple inches taller than she was, Jessica guessed. But with a body like that and a face to match, height didn't seem important. Obviously he'd gotten himself cleaned up since she'd first seen him. His longish, light-brown hair was slightly damp and neatly combed. He was wearing a shirt now, to Jessica's disappointment—a light-blue denim one that enhanced his broad shoulders and tanned

30

neck. But the tight-fitting jeans were the same.

He caught Jessica's eye and smiled—a wide grin that melted something deep inside her.

"Liz!" she whispered. "He's coming over here."

"Well, howdy, girls!" the cowboy said, holding out his hand to Jessica. "Scott Culver is the name. I noticed you two driving by on I-15 a ways back, after my car broke down. The tow-truck driver said it was two pretty blond girls in a Jeep who told him I needed help. Thank you kindly for sending him back for me."

He laughed. "You know, I thought you were some sort of mirage at first—it didn't seem possible for two beautiful women to look so much alike. You really are absolutely identical, aren't you?"

"I'm Jessica Wakefield, and this is my sister, Elizabeth," Jessica said. "As soon as you get to know us, you won't have any trouble seeing how different we are."

"I sure wouldn't mind the chance to discover that for myself."

Jessica pulled her skirt closer to clear a space on the bench beside her. "Why don't you join us?" She ignored a glare from Elizabeth. "We're students from Sweet Valley University, on our way to Vail for a skiing trip. But right now, we were just about to have a piece of pie."

Scott slid into the booth. He wasn't quite

touching her, but he was sitting so close in the tiny booth that Jessica thought she could feel the heat from his leg against hers.

The waitress clicked over on her high heels and set two pieces of pie and two more sodas in front of the girls. "Can I get you anything, sir?" she asked.

Scott flashed another grin, and Jessica saw the waitress's eyes light up. Only Elizabeth seemed immune to Scott's charms. And Jessica was sure even she would warm up to him, as soon as she saw that he wasn't some sort of homicidal fugitive.

"Sure," Scott told the waitress. "That pie looks awfully good. I'll have a piece of blueberry—and a cherry cola. And I'll take care of the check for my two lovely friends here."

"Pay up at the register whenever you're ready," the waitress said, handing him the bill. "I'll be back with your blueberry pie in a minute."

Elizabeth tried to grab the check from him, but Scott held it out of her reach. "Scott, you don't have to pay that," she told him.

"Are you kidding? I insist. It's the least I can do for two angels of mercy like yourselves. You don't know how grateful I am to you for sending that tow truck. I could've been stuck in that infernal desert all night!"

Jessica almost sighed out loud. What a gentleman! And what a smile. She had never seen teeth so white and even.

"So where were you heading, Scott?" Elizabeth asked. Her voice was polite and friendly, but Jessica knew her well enough to detect a trace of suspicion in it.

"I'm on winter break from school," he said. "I was on my way to Vail to work on the slopes over vacation, when my car died."

"What a coincidence!" Jessica exclaimed. "As I said, we're going there, too."

Scott's sexy gray eyes widened. "Oh, did you say Vail? I must have been distracted. It didn't even register."

Jessica felt herself blushing at the way he gazed into her eyes when he said the word *distracted*.

"You said you go to school?" Elizabeth asked, raising her eyebrows.

"First-year med school," Scott said. "I'm at the University of California, San Francisco campus."

"So you're not a cowboy?" Jessica asked, a little disappointed.

"Well, I did live in Montana for the last two years, before I started med school." He pointed to the hat. "And I do own a Stetson and cowboy boots. But frankly, I wouldn't know one end of a horse from the other."

He grinned again, and Jessica's disappointment faded. Horses were smelly, anyway.

"You say you lived in Montana for two years," Elizabeth said, staring at him intently. "If you're a first-year med student now, you must have been an undergraduate then, right?"

Scott returned her stare. Elizabeth's gaze looked suspicious, Jessica thought, while Scott's was perfectly open and friendly. The waitress set a slice of blueberry pie and a soda in front of him. "I graduated from Montana State University, in Bozeman," he said. "Class of last June. Before that, I spent two years in a community college."

Jessica glared at Elizabeth. Scott had definitely won this round of the third degree. "I told you so," Jessica mouthed, furious. Elizabeth had no right to treat someone as sexy as Scott like a criminal. A change of subject was definitely in order. "What did the mechanic say about your car?" she asked him with a smile.

"If it was a horse, I'd have to shoot it. Unless I want to spend a fortune to put a whole new radiator into a car that's already fifteen years old."·

Jessica was crestfallen. "So you're not going to Vail?"

Scott shook his head. "Oh, I can't give up on Vail; I need the dough to pay my tuition for next semester. But I have it all worked out. It'll take me an extra day, but I can get to Vail by bus. The tow-truck driver said there's one that comes through here tonight."

Suddenly Jessica had a wonderful idea. She would get to spend a lot more time with Scott—

and she would have the best-looking date at the New Year's Eve party. She felt excitement rising inside her. Then she remembered her twin.

Elizabeth had a thoughtful look on her face as she swallowed a mouthful of her cherry pie. Jessica recognized her twin's gaze. It was Elizabeth's investigative-reporter-hot-on-a-story look, perfected through years of working on the high school newspaper and now on SVU's television station. Apparently, Elizabeth thought she was on the trail of a major exposé.

"There's one thing I just don't understand, Scott," began Elizabeth Wakefield, girl reporter. "Why would you come this far south on a trip from San Francisco to Vail? Most people would've gone through Reno and across central Nevada."

Scott smiled again, and Jessica felt her heart jump in her chest at the sight of his wide, sensuous mouth. "Is that so?" He laughed. "Geography was never one of my strong subjects. I guess that's why I decided on medical school. But seriously, I just spent the holiday with my roommate's family in Bakersfield. This seemed to be the quickest route from there."

Jessica grinned. Elizabeth looked properly chastised.

"Well, if you lovely ladies are finished here, I'll take care of the bill."

Jessica watched the back of his jeans as he

sauntered up to the counter. "Wow! What a body!"

"Jessica, you were practically sitting in his lap."

"I can't help it if it's a small booth. Besides, he didn't seem to mind. Come on, Liz. Let's offer Scott a ride to Vail. It's silly for him to sit in a hot, smelly bus for two days when we're going to the same place. Bringing him along wouldn't be any inconvenience at all."

"I swear, Jess, sometimes I think you have popcorn for brains. We don't know anything about him."

"We know that your worst suspicions were wrong. He doesn't sound like a psychopath who's escaped from death row." She cast an admiring glance at Scott's lean frame. "And he sure doesn't look like one."

"I don't know, Jess. I don't like the idea of letting a stranger into our car. He seems like a nice guy, but—"

"Of course he's a nice guy! Look at the way he insisted on paying the bill for us! He's a med student, for pete's sake! Besides, he's not a stranger—we just had a nice, long talk with him. *You* couldn't even find anything wrong with him."

"That's true," Elizabeth admitted. "Everything he said sounded perfectly reasonable."

"So what's the problem? What happened to Elizabeth Wakefield, Friend to People in Need?

Come on, Liz! Please, please, please?"

Elizabeth laughed. "You look like Prince Albert begging for a doggy snack!"

Jessica gave her sister her best imploring look.

Elizabeth shook her head, chuckling. "All right, all right! I guess you can ask Scott if he wants to ride with us."

"Thanks, Elizabeth. You won't regret it."

"Uh-oh."

"What now?"

"That's what you always say when I agree to something I end up regretting."

"Believe me, I know this guy," Jeff Marks insisted to the local sheriff and his deputy. The men were gathered just outside the door of the tiny service station north of Tonovah, Nevada. "It's the same guy who held up a convenience store near Eureka yesterday."

"I'm not one to argue with the FBI," said the overweight sheriff. Jeff noticed that his teeth were stained brown. "But I don't see any evidence of that."

"We have plenty of evidence," Jeff lied. "The Bureau is certain that the robberies are related."

"The Bureau ain't certain of a darn thing," the deputy said in an accusing voice. "You got no suspect. You don't even got no witnesses."

The sheriff took Jeff's arm companionably. "Listen here, young man," he said in an overly reasonable voice, as if he were talking to an uncomprehending child. "Stores are held up all the time, all over the state."

Jeff wrenched his arm free. "Two people are dead!"

"So they are," the sheriff continued. "And it's a damn shame. But what's one little armed robbery in Tonovah to the FBI? Frankly, I don't even see why the Feds are involved."

"Yup," the deputy agreed. "Looks like a local case to me, too."

Jeff sighed. It was always a hard sell with these small-town law-enforcement officials. A place like Tonovah probably had a serious crime once every five years. When a violent crime did come along, the local cops saw their chance to work on a real case, win a few medals, and maybe put their department on the map. Admitting that this robbery and shooting could be part of an interstate chain of incidents would be like handing the case over to the FBI on a silver platter.

"We've been tracking a series of similar crimes over the last month," Jeff explained, trying to keep the impatience out of his voice. "The perpetrator crossed state lines, so it's a federal matter."

"So, this small-time scum—excuse me, I mean this *perpetrator* is a federal matter, is he?" the sheriff said.

Jeff chastised himself silently. He knew better

than to use a word like perpetrator with these small-town officials.

The deputy grinned. His teeth were crooked. "Things must be awful slow for the FBI these days, to send a college boy like you out to little old Tonovah to check out a small-time store heist."

"Show some respect, Clem," the sheriff admonished. "I bet this *perpetrator* is the biggest threat to the Feds since Al Capone. Tonovah attracts nothing but the best, you know."

Jeff rolled his eyes. "Obviously."

The sheriff spat a stream of tobacco juice. "You said this all-important *perpetrator's* been across state lines. I bet he's robbed convenience stores all the way from Washington, D.C.!"

Jeff gritted his teeth and resolved not to lose his temper. "Utah, actually," he admitted. "First there was a string of holdups in Utah. They were mostly convenience stores and gas stations—usually on secondary roads, in small towns and rural areas. Before Utah, we have reports of similar crimes in Wyoming, and even as far away as Montana."

"I knew it!" the deputy said. "Sounds like Jesse James and his gang."

Jeff ignored him. "The trail is too cold on the Wyoming and Montana incidents. But I'm sure the Utah holdups fit in with the pattern. And in the last couple weeks, Nevada's been hit hard:

Wendover, Tuscarora, Gerlach, Stillwater, Eureka, and now here. And those are only the ones I'm sure of."

"Doesn't sound to me like you're sure of much, for a college boy," the sheriff said with a sneer.

"I tell you, this guy is crisscrossing the state. He's robbing stores and leaving people dead—or in no shape to talk. It's time to find some answers."

The sheriff spat a stream of tobacco juice. "This guy?" he repeated. "Sounds like you've got all the answers already, Mr. FBI. From what I hear of those cases, there's no telling whether it was a guy or a girl or a whole gang of juvenile delinquents."

"If you'll just hear me out—"

"I think you city slickers from the Fed ought to go back to Washington where you came from," the sheriff interrupted, an icy look in his eyes. "And leave law enforcement to the people who know the area."

Jeff felt his face go as red as the sunset. "Dammit! I was born and raised in Carson City!"

The deputy and sheriff exchanged an amused glance. "So the Fed's got a temper," drawled the deputy.

Jeff berated himself silently. He'd never get their cooperation if he kept losing his cool. "Look,

I've been studying these cases for a long time. I have a degree in criminal psychology, and I believe the perpetrator is a male, probably Caucasian. And I believe he's working alone."

He went on in a thoughtful tone, almost forgetting that he had an audience. "He does it for the money, of course. But it's also a power thing. This guy feels a rush of power when he victimizes somebody he sees as weaker than he is."

"If it's all one guy, then how do you explain the different guns?" the sheriff asked.

"A few of the victims were hit by the same gun—but not in the same state, until now. And all four of the guns he's used were stolen." Jeff stared up at Tonovah Summit, shaded in swaths of coral and amber by the rays of the setting sun.

"Sounds like one smart dude," the deputy drawled.

"He is smart," Jeff agreed. "He's too smart to leave witnesses, or any evidence at all. So he kills. Some of the victims could have hit a silent alarm and didn't. So he was able to get close without frightening them—until it was too late. That would suggest a normal, even friendly demeanor."

"He don't sound too normal to me," the sheriff pointed out.

"He's not," Jeff continued in the same intense voice, still staring at the darkening mountain. "This guy is anything but normal. He's a cold, calculating killer who shows no remorse."

41

Jeff stared at the mountain for another few seconds, thinking of Summer O'Brian. Then he remembered the sheriff and deputy. They were grinning at him as if he'd lost his mind. He felt his face go pink.

The sheriff spat another long stream of tobacco juice. "Those university degrees in criminal psychology sure are something, aren't they?" he asked the deputy. "Hard to believe he can tell all that—after just twenty minutes of looking at nothing but a coroner's report, some playing cards on the floor, and a bullet dug out of a telephone. You got to hand it to these fellows from the FBI."

"You know these city boys," the deputy remarked. "They're smart—real smart."

Jeff gritted his teeth and swore to himself that he would act cool and professional. "I know the bullet from this morning's holdup was from a Colt .45," he said, trying not to sound defensive. "That's the same kind of weapon used in the Stillwater incident. Now I'll take what's left of the bullet back to the lab and see if it's from the same gun."

"I don't know about that," the sheriff said. "That bullet is evidence. Seems to me it ought to stay right here in Tonovah, where this investigation is taking place."

Jeff gripped the man's arm. "I don't mean to impede your local investigation. All I'm asking is that you don't impede mine."

"Then go back to the state capital," suggested the sheriff.

"You don't have a lab here like the one the FBI has in Carson City. We'll analyze the bullet there. Then I'll send you a complete report of whatever we learn about it. And I also expect you to share any evidence you find with the FBI."

The sheriff smiled, showing off his brown-stained teeth. He dropped into Jeff's hand a small plastic bag containing the bullet fragment. "As I said before, I'm not one to argue with the FBI."

"Absolutely not!" Scott said as he and the twins walked out of the diner into the fading light of the desert. "You girls have already put yourselves out for me. I couldn't accept a ride all the way to Vail. I mean, you don't even know me."

Elizabeth felt her suspicions melting. Surely, somebody with dishonest intentions would have accepted a ride instantly. "Really, Scott," she said, "it's no inconvenience at all."

Jessica threw her a grateful glance. "That's right, Scott. You're going to the exact same place as us. All we'll have to do is shift my luggage around a little, and we can fit you in the backseat, no problem."

"No, it's too much of an imposition. You didn't sign on for this when you told the tow-truck driver about me. I can't take advantage of your kindness that way."

43

"It's no imposition!" Jessica insisted brightly. "You can protect us from all the homicidal maniacs out on the road."

Scott shook his head. "No, really. I appreciate the kind sentiments, but I don't mind taking the bus."

Elizabeth couldn't help smiling back at his guileless grin. "Please, Scott. We insist."

Scott looked from one twin to the other. "All right, I'll accept your offer—but on one condition. You have to let me pay for the gas."

Jessica's eyes lit up, but Elizabeth had to protest. "No way! We'd have to pay for our gas anyhow. There's no reason why you should pay it all. At the most, we'll let you split it."

Scott shook his head. "No deal. You two are kind enough to offer me a ride, so I plan to do my part. I had enough cash with me to fuel that broken-down guzzler I was driving. Your Jeep probably gets twice the gas mileage. I insist on paying for the gas."

Elizabeth couldn't resist his boyish grin. Jessica was right; Scott was incredibly handsome. And his offer was enticing. Five hundred dollars for each twin had seemed like a lot. But it would disappear quickly as soon as they started to rent skis and buy lift tickets—not to mention food and lodging for a week at a fancy ski resort. Not having to worry about gas money would be a relief.

"All right. It's a deal," Elizabeth said. Jessica looked as if she were about to jump for joy. And Scott's smile grew wider. Elizabeth sighed. "Why do I feel as if I've been giving in to people all day, against my better judgment?"

"You're just a giving person," said Jessica. But her eyes were on Scott's handsome face.

Jeff stood in front of the service station north of Tonovah and watched the sheriff's car meander down the road, toward the half-darkened summit. Why was he the only law-enforcement official in the state who felt any sense of urgency about catching this criminal? He shook his head, knowing the answer but not wanting to think about it.

He yanked open the door of his Mustang and climbed inside. Summer had always teased him about the car. She said it wasn't the kind of car people expected an FBI agent to drive. But at twenty-six years old, he felt too young for the big-black-sedan routine. He could always use one of the Bureau's dark, plain cars when he needed something less conspicuous for undercover work. And he knew that Summer had loved his Mustang almost as much as he did.

He lifted her photograph and cradled it in his hands. God, she was beautiful, with her black hair and warm blue eyes. More important than that, she was brilliant, creative, and full of life.

Summer O'Brian had been a gourmet chef, a hang-gliding enthusiast, and a graduate student in Native American history. She had meant everything to Jeff. The happiest day of his life had been the day, a few months earlier, when she'd agreed to be his wife. Now he would never see her again.

Ten nights earlier, Summer had stopped to eat at a diner near Stillwater, Nevada. It was late on a rainy weeknight, and she was the only customer. At least, the police assumed she was the only customer. The waitress was in a coma and not expected to recover. And no other witnesses were left alive—except for a passing motorist who remembered a blue sedan in the parking lot. When the police arrived, the cash register had been cleaned out. And a barrage of gunfire from a Colt .45 had ended Summer's life.

"Gone," Jeff whispered to the woman in the photograph. A handful of cash and a quick getaway had been the payoff—in exchange for a living, breathing, beautiful human being. A human being he had loved with all his heart. Jeff had seen death before. But identifying his fiancée's body at the Churchill County morgue was the most difficult task he'd ever had to do. He'd vowed then that he would find the person who had murdered her. He wouldn't feel at peace until the killer was behind bars—or was lying in the morgue, as dead as Summer.

Jeff renewed his vow now, pounding a fist against the steering wheel of the Mustang. He couldn't bring Summer back. But he could keep her killer from cutting down another young, innocent woman who had everything to live for.

Chapter Three

Elizabeth was about to pull open the passenger-side door of the Jeep when Jessica stopped her. "You seem a little tired, Liz. I think it would help you wake up if I let you take my turn to drive for a while."

"Oh, really? How generous of you to think of me."

"You know me!" Jessica said with a shrug. "Generous to a fault."

Elizabeth recognized the entreaty in her sister's eyes. Jessica was pleading for a chance to spend some time with Scott.

Elizabeth laughed and shook her head. "Fault is right. Okay, I'll drive. But why does this remind me of the way you always get me to clean your side of the room at school?"

Jessica shrugged again, as if she had no idea what Elizabeth meant. Then she turned to survey the luggage—most of it her own—that was strewn across the backseat. "Now how will we fit him in?"

"You can put some of our luggage behind the seat," Elizabeth suggested.

"Not all of it will fit back there," Jessica complained.

"So, leave a suitcase or two on the backseat. Scott won't mind sharing with them."

Jessica shook her head. "No. The only way we can make room for another person is to move these two suitcases to the *front* seat. Don't you think they'll fit better there, Liz?"

Jessica's eyes were twinkling, and Elizabeth knew what she was getting at. "Sure, Jess," she agreed. "But do you think the two of you will be comfortable on that little backseat?"

Jessica began moving the suitcases. "Don't you worry about me and Scott. We'll fit somehow."

"Is that duffel bag all you're bringing with you for a whole month at Vail, Scott?" Elizabeth asked.

"I'll never understand men," Jessica declared. "I brought about six times as much stuff, and I'm only going for one week!" She reached for the bag. "Let me get it for you, Scott. I've made the perfect space for it here on the front seat."

Scott yanked the bag away from her. "No, thanks, Jessica! I'm kind of used to having it with me. It'll fit just fine on the floor, under my knees."

"Are you sure? We may be a little crowded back there as it is."

Scott gazed into Jessica's eyes, and Elizabeth felt a stab of misgiving at the look of adoration on her sister's face.

"I don't mind a little togetherness, if you don't," Scott said in a husky voice.

"No," she said. "I don't mind at all."

Elizabeth wondered if she should throw a bucket of cold water on them both. Then she had a better idea. "You know, guys, now that it's cooler out, it's really a beautiful night. Let's put the top down—it'll keep you two from feeling claustrophobic back there."

"Great idea!" Jessica exclaimed. "Don't you just love convertibles?"

A half hour later, Elizabeth turned the Jeep off the road, just over the Nevada border, and pulled it into a gas station. "I can't believe I was so dumb," she said. "We were stopped for all that time right across the street from a service station. And we never once thought to get gas!"

"All's well that ends well," Jessica said. It wasn't like Elizabeth to forget something like putting gas in the car, she thought. Then again, Elizabeth had been awfully busy at the time, trying to make sure that adorable, sexy Scott wasn't a chain-saw murderer or a vampire or something.

"I'll fill the tank," Scott offered, jumping out of the Jeep without opening the door.

"Thanks, Scott," Elizabeth said with a grateful smile. "That'll give me a chance to make a phone call. My overprotective boyfriend is expecting a call soon to say we're in Utah and have stopped for the night. I'll have to break the news to him that we're not going to make it that far."

"Utah?" Scott asked. "I didn't know you were going to Utah."

"Just passing through," Elizabeth said as she fished in her purse for some change. "Take a look at the map if you want. The route to Vail goes right through the central part of the state."

Scott laughed. "It's a good thing one of us can read a map. As I said, I'm crummy at geography."

"Join the club," Jessica said. "My family always says I need a compass and a map to find my way to the kitchen."

"Only when it's your turn to make dinner," Elizabeth called over her shoulder as she headed for the telephone.

Jessica sighed dramatically. "Why couldn't I be an only child?"

"You may not be an only child, but you're certainly one of a kind," Scott said, leaning over the side of the Jeep. Jessica's heart melted as he lifted her hand in his and gently kissed it. He whipped off his hat and perched it on Jessica's head. Then he reached for the gas pump.

What a way to start a vacation, she thought as soon as she could get her brain working again. *This guy is incredible!* From under the brim of the Stetson, Jessica watched Scott's lean, muscular body as he lifted the nozzle and started pumping gas into the Jeep. She couldn't wait to tell Isabella all about him. Then she remembered she would be introducing him to Isabella at the New Year's Eve party the very next night—after she showed up at the ski resort with the hottest guy in the West. *I wonder if there's any way I can arrange to stay in Colorado for a whole month.*

Elizabeth tried to keep her mind on what Tom was saying to her. But she couldn't help watching her sister from the phone booth across the parking lot. Scott was pumping gas. And Jessica, wearing Scott's cowboy hat, was gazing at him adoringly.

"What, Tom?" Elizabeth said guiltily into the phone, realizing he had asked her a question. "No. We haven't stopped for the night yet."

"Is there a problem? Are you having car trouble?"

"No, we're fine. But Jessica wanted to hit every convenience store in California for root beer fill-ups."

"I should have guessed it was Jessica holding things up."

"Then we took a break at a diner a little before the Nevada border," Elizabeth explained apologetically.

"We kind of lost track of the time and stayed longer than we should have—what with Jessica wanting to eat a piece of pie, and then convincing me to give Scott a ride—"

"Scott?" Tom asked, instantly on alert. "Who the heck is Scott?"

"Scott Culver. He's a med student we met along the way. He was heading to Vail, too, and his car broke down. So he's riding with us."

Elizabeth could hear disapproval in her boyfriend's voice. "I don't know about this, Liz. Do you really think it's wise to give a lift to a perfect stranger? I mean, what do you know about him?"

"I know that Jessica is so infatuated with him that she can hardly see straight."

"And we all know what an excellent judge of character Jessica is when it comes to guys."

"Come on, Tom. You know I wouldn't have offered him a ride if I wasn't sure he was all right—no matter how hard Jessica begged."

"I know. But I still don't like it."

Elizabeth was getting sick of his overprotectiveness. "Tom, you're being paranoid."

"I know. I'm so used to protecting you from crazy fraternity guys and secret society members that I guess I miss being your knight in shining armor."

"I wasn't the only reporter cracking those stories," Elizabeth reminded him. "I was only the

54

intern. *You* were the senior correspondent."

"Right. So I know exactly how much danger you were in. And I just heard a pretty scary report on the radio. There's been a string of armed robberies in convenience stores and gas stations across Nevada."

"Tom, if there really are dangerous criminals around, don't you think we'd be safer with a man in the car?"

"Only if it were me." Tom sighed. "I guess so. I'm sorry, Liz. I know I'm being silly. Just promise me you'll be careful—don't take any chances with this med student. The minute your gut instinct tells you something's wrong, I want you to dump him at the next rest stop and get out of there—no matter what Jessica says."

"I promise!" Elizabeth said. Tom's fear was contagious. She suddenly found herself looking over her shoulder, scrutinizing Scott as he sauntered into the station to pay for the gas. He was wearing his hat again, and his old canvas duffel bag swung near his knees.

Elizabeth consciously pushed Tom's anxiety out of her mind. Even if she was a little nervous about having a stranger in the car, there was no reason to get Tom any more worried than he already was.

"Anyway, I mostly called to tell you that I don't think we'll make it to Utah tonight. We should get somewhere past Vegas. If I can roust

Jessica out of bed and get a super-early start to-morrow, we'll still be in Vail in time for the New Year's Eve party."

"I'll save every dance for you."

"You'd better!"

Elizabeth hung up the phone and walked back to the Jeep, lost in thought. Tom had a point. No matter how nice a guy Scott was, she had to be insane to give a ride to a perfect stranger. Maybe she was the one with popcorn for brains. If she had any intelligence at all, she would jump into the driver's seat and zoom off toward Las Vegas, leaving Scott inside.

But there was Jessica, sitting in the Jeep with a dreamy expression on her face. *She's had a rough semester,* Elizabeth reminded herself. *If flirting with a med student for a day or two makes her this happy, who am I to get in the way?*

She sighed. Whether Tom liked it or not, it seemed that the twins had acquired an extra passenger for the trip to Vail.

Jessica smiled, remembering the feel of Scott's dry, soft lips on the back of her hand. And now he was inside, paying for their gas. Scott was part gentleman, part cowboy, part skier, part serious medical student, and one hundred percent gorgeous.

But here was Elizabeth, walking toward her across the pavement. The parking lot was dim, but

56

not dim enough to mask the unsettled expression on Elizabeth's face. *Oh, no,* thought Jessica. *That's the look of a woman whose boyfriend has just given her a stern warning about picking up stranded strangers.* Then Elizabeth's face softened, and Jessica recognized the look of a sister who wanted her to be happy. She grinned back. "How's Tom?"

"Acting like Dad," Elizabeth admitted as she climbed into the front seat. "Is Scott still paying for the gas? He's been in there quite a while."

"Yes, he has," Jessica realized. "Maybe he had to use the bathroom." Then she spotted a worn leather wallet on the seat beside her. "Oh, no! He left his wallet in the car. I guess I'd better bring it to him, or he won't be able to pay."

"Don't bother," Elizabeth said. "Here he comes now. He must have had some money in that duffel bag."

Sure enough, Scott stood at the door of the gas station. He turned back to wave to the attendant inside. "And you have a nice day, too, sir!" he called in a jovial tone.

Then he ambled toward the Jeep, flashing Jessica a heart-stopping smile that seemed to light up the whole parking lot.

A minute later, Elizabeth started the Jeep. "Maybe I'd better run in before we leave and use the bathroom, too," Jessica said suddenly. "That way, we won't have to stop again for a while. I'll be right back."

"No!" Scott said quickly. "I mean, you can't. It's out of order."

"Oh, well," Jessica said. "I guess I can wait."

Tom folded the Los Angeles newspaper and laid it on the desk in his dorm room. Also on the desk were two framed photos. The picture he treasured the most was of Elizabeth, standing in front of a camcorder to tape her first on-camera news story, the one that exposed the campus secret society and put her life in danger. The other photograph was of Tom's idols, Bob Woodward and Carl Bernstein, the investigative reporters who cracked the Watergate case for the *Washington Post*.

He wished the two famous reporters were in Nevada right now. If the news reports were any indication, the police and the FBI needed all the help they could get with stopping the string of armed robberies across the state. So far, there were no witnesses and no survivors who were in any shape to talk about what had happened.

He shook his head. "Liz is right," he said aloud. "I'm being silly. Nevada's a big state—the fact that a few convenience stores have been knocked off doesn't mean that she and Jessica are in any danger. True, she's crazy to offer a ride all the way to Colorado to a complete stranger. But Liz is a good judge of character. I'll see her tomorrow night in Vail, and everything will be fine."

He gently lifted Elizabeth's picture and stared into her clear blue-green eyes. He desperately hoped that he was right.

Elizabeth squinted into the deepening twilight before remembering to switch on the headlights. She steered the Jeep along the interstate, heading north toward the outskirts of Las Vegas. The night air was mild. The wind swept through her hair, a welcome relief from the heat of the day.

Elizabeth sighed. The desert scenery was beautiful at this time of evening, in a haunting sort of way. Rock formations glowed red, reflecting a few renegade rays of sunlight. The tall, otherworldly shapes of Joshua trees showed like black spears against the lighter black of the sky. If Elizabeth had been alone, she would have liked to stop and immerse herself in the landscape—maybe even write a poem.

But this was no time for solitude. Las Vegas, nightlife capital of the West, was only a few miles ahead. Tom's warnings had raised vague fears in Elizabeth's mind. But Jessica's exuberant mood was hard to resist. She and Scott were singing along with the radio as loudly as they could.

Elizabeth erupted into giggles. "Scott," she called loudly, so that her voice would carry over the never-ending rush of air that swept the open Jeep. "I didn't think it was possible, but you sing even worse than Jessica!"

He laughed. "So you're saying I shouldn't quit medical school to open at Caesars any time soon?"

"Exactly." Elizabeth remembered Tom's warnings again, and decided to prove to herself that she had nothing to worry about. "Tell me more about school, Scott," she ventured. "What classes did you take in your first semester?"

"For one, you are speaking with a veteran of the dreaded an-phys."

Jessica grimaced. "Sounds like an antacid tablet."

"Almost," Scott said. "It's shorthand for first-year anatomy and physiology. It's the great weeder-outer of the unprepared, the unsuspecting—"

"And the unintelligent," Jessica added.

Scott laughed. "Also the unsadistic. Dissections are required in an-phys; no conscientious objectors are tolerated."

Jessica wrinkled her nose. "Ugh! What did you have to cut up?"

"Believe me, you'd rather not know. Besides, I shouldn't be discussing anatomically correct amphibians in mixed company."

"I take it you passed," Elizabeth said, with a slight question in her voice.

"Actually, I pulled a *B*," Scott said. "Not too shabby, if I do say so myself."

"When you're through with med school, what kind of medicine do you plan to practice?"

Scott cocked his head. "I haven't exactly made up my mind yet, Liz," he said apologetically. "But I'm thinking of becoming an otolaryngologist."

Elizabeth nodded, impressed. Scott certainly did seem to know his stuff. "An ENT."

Jessica narrowed her eyes. "A what-agologist?"

"You know," Scott said, playfully tweaking her nose, "an ear-nose-and-throat man."

"I would've pegged you as more of a leg man," Jessica responded mischievously. Elizabeth watched in the rearview mirror as Jessica's right leg just barely brushed against Scott's left one. Looking at Jessica's face, Elizabeth was sure the brief contact had been no accident. Scott smiled slyly at Jessica and wrapped an arm around her shoulders.

Elizabeth was dismayed by her sister's behavior. Obviously, Scott was exactly what he claimed to be—a medical student with a dead car. But that was no reason for Jessica to come on to a guy she'd just met. Scott was charming, but he was still a stranger. And the twins would be spending the entire next day with him, at close quarters.

She tried to catch Jessica's eye in the rearview mirror to transmit a glare full of sisterly disapproval. Jessica didn't even look up.

"Jessica tells me you're a writer, Elizabeth," Scott said. "You know, that's quite a talent to have. I've always wished I were inspired by that particular Muse."

61

A wave of guilt washed over Elizabeth. *How could I have been so suspicious of this sweet, likable guy?* She decided to make it up to him. "If you're smart enough to be in medical school, I'm sure you could write if you set your mind to it."

"No. That's a skill I just don't have," Scott said. "I have to content myself with reading the works of those with more talent."

"Oh? Which authors do you like?"

"Quite a variety," Scott said. "I especially like to read authors' works and then learn something about their personal lives. I find it adds a whole new context to the literature. For instance, did you know that Chekhov himself started as a physician?"

"Check who?" Jessica asked.

"Did he really?" Elizabeth asked. "I saw a production of *The Cherry Orchard* at school last semester. What a powerful play!"

"Puh-lease!" Jessica urged. "This is beginning to sound like a literature lecture. I thought we were traveling to get away from all that! Let's do something wild and crazy and impulsive! I never get to do anything fun."

Elizabeth laughed. "Ha! Since when?"

"I have a feeling that you manage to have fun in just about any situation," Scott said. "But I do have a suggestion; that is, if you think it sounds reasonable, Liz."

Jessica slumped in her seat with a pretty pout.

"If Liz thinks it sounds reasonable, I doubt it could be much fun."

Scott caught Elizabeth's eye in the rearview mirror. "You know, Las Vegas is surprisingly inexpensive if you're not a gambler. Why don't we stop at one of the big, glitzy hotels for the night? Of course, you two aren't old enough to be allowed on the casino floor. But we could get some dinner, look at the lights, and just kind of soak up the ambience."

Jessica's eyes were shining, and Elizabeth had to admit that the idea was tempting. "I don't know," she said, already noticing the glow of the city on the horizon ahead. "We really ought to get as far as possible tonight. We could keep going for another hour, easily."

"And then find ourselves stuck in a desert, dead tired, without a motel in sight," Scott reminded her. "Nevada's pretty sparsely populated, compared to what you girls are used to in California. We might not be able to find a hotel with a vacancy when we decide we're ready to stop."

"Please, Liz?" Jessica cajoled. "Pretty please?"

Elizabeth rolled her eyes.

"Come on, Elizabeth! You've never been to Vegas either—don't tell me you aren't the least bit curious about it. And besides, we're not even old enough to gamble. So what trouble could we possibly get into?"

"Sorry to be a stick-in-the-mud," Elizabeth said. "But somebody has to play the responsible adult, Jessica. I'm just worried that we won't make it to Vail in time to meet Tom and Danny and Isabella tomorrow night."

"How many miles is it from Vegas to Vail?" Scott asked.

Elizabeth picked up the map and glanced briefly at the notes she'd written in the margin. "Six hundred and fifty."

"I may be lousy at maps, but math I can do," Scott said. "Say we head out of Vegas by seven o'clock in the morning. If we stop only when necessary, and if we eat in the car, we can be still be in Vail by eight at night. What time are you supposed to meet your friends?"

"That's fantastic!" Jessica exclaimed. "Liz, the party doesn't start until nine thirty! That'll give us time to check into the hotel and get dressed."

Elizabeth smiled, beginning to feel a little adventurous herself. "Okay. Let's do it!"

Suddenly Jessica sighed despondently.

Elizabeth was instantly suspicious. She was used to her sister's abrupt mood swings, but this jump was a little too quick, even for Jessica. Elizabeth was sure her sister had something up her sleeve.

"What's the matter?" asked Scott, his husky voice full of concern. Elizabeth felt a little sorry for him. After eighteen years of Jessica's schemes, she had a pretty good idea of when her sister was trying to manipulate someone. Scott was about to be Jessica'd, and he didn't even know it.

"Oh, it's nothing," Jessica said in her tearful-but-brave voice.

"Come on, Jessica," he urged gently. "You can tell me what's bothering you."

Jessica sighed again. "It isn't important, really. It's just that we'll be arriving so late that I won't have time to find a date for the party. But I'm sure I'll have a good time anyway. Elizabeth and Isabella won't mind if their boyfriends dance with me once or twice."

Elizabeth rolled her eyes. Jessica had Scott exactly where she wanted him.

"I'm no Fred Astaire," Scott began, "but any man would look graceful dancing with you, Jessica. I'd be happy to take you to that New Year's Eve party—that is, if you won't mind being seen with a klutz like me."

Elizabeth stifled an urge to laugh. *Mind? From the moment Jessica heard Scott was going to Vail, she's been imagining herself gliding into that party on his arm.* Elizabeth had been worried all along about Scott being dangerous somehow. Now she realized her fears were misplaced. It was Scott who was in danger, she decided. No man could last long against the wiles of Jessica Wakefield.

*   *   *

65

The Jeep rolled off the interstate and into Las Vegas.

"This is so cool!" Jessica gasped, gazing in wonder at the lights of the Strip. Every surface on every building seemed to be covered with neon, so that the entire street glittered in the night like precious jewels against black velvet. "I didn't know there were this many lights in the entire world! Slow down, Liz, so we can see them all."

Elizabeth whistled as she slowed the Jeep to a crawl. "I bet even Lila would have trouble handling the electric bill for just one night of all this!"

Jessica turned to Scott. "Lila's my best friend from high school," she explained. "She's a millionaire."

Scott nodded, his face overlaid with the shifting colors of thousands of gleaming, flashing, rotating, and exploding bulbs. "Nice work if you can get it."

"Wow! Look at that!" Jessica said, pointing to a huge structure on the left. "It looks just like a castle." Its walls were smooth white, lit with a glacial blue light that made its many turrets glow as if they were enchanted.

"It looks like something out of a storybook," Elizabeth said, entranced. "I wonder what it is!"

"The Excalibur," Scott said. "It's a hotel and casino—like practically everything else on the Strip."

"That's the Tropicana across the street!" Jessica

yelled, pointing. "I've heard of that one! I can't believe we're really seeing all these famous hotels."

Elizabeth went on talking with Scott, as if Jessica hadn't spoken. "You know Vegas well?" she asked, sounding as if she were fishing for information again.

Jessica tuned out her sister and instead admired the way the reflections of the lights rolled and swerved and stretched along the shiny black surface of the Jeep as it moved down the Strip.

Scott shrugged. "I wouldn't say I know it *well*. But I have been through here a couple times. It's a pretty wild place. Did you know they've got slot machines absolutely everywhere—even in the Laundromats?"

"Wow! There's a hotel that looks like a humongous green pyramid!" Jessica exclaimed. "It's even got a sphinx on the side. How totally cool!"

"Look on the left," Elizabeth urged, distracted again from the subject of Scott's background. "Neon palm trees!"

"The Dunes," Scott supplied.

"And there's Caesars Palace!" Jessica called, gesturing frantically toward the next hotel. "Look at all the statues and the fountains. I'm going to die. I can't believe I'm actually in front of Caesars Palace! It must be the most famous hotel in the world. Oh, can we stay there, please?"

Elizabeth shrugged. "Anywhere you want—

providing we can afford it. But let's drive along the rest of the Strip first."

Jessica screamed.

"What is it?" Elizabeth asked, trying to see her from the driver's seat without taking her eyes off the road.

"A volcano! Look at it! A volcano just erupted in front of that hotel! This is the wildest thing I've ever seen in my life."

Elizabeth gasped, and Jessica knew she had caught sight of the large hotel, set back from the Strip. In front of it an enormous diorama looked exactly like a volcanic island somewhere in the South Pacific. An artificial lake glowed with orange light, reflecting real flames from an erupting volcano on a rocky island in the center.

Scott reached over to hold Jessica's hand. She turned to smile at him and was momentarily startled. The blaze from the volcano reflected, blood red, on his handsome features, forming a mask that was almost demonic. Then Scott flashed her one of his devastatingly gorgeous smiles, and the illusion disappeared.

"The one with the volcano is called the Mirage," Elizabeth said. "This whole town is like a mirage! I'd heard Vegas was glitzy, but I never imagined anything like this!"

Scott nodded. "The place can be overwhelming the first time you drive through it at night."

Jessica laughed, catching sight of a pair of

gilded arches rising against the black sky. "Even the fast-food places are covered with neon! I love Las Vegas! This is going to be an awesome night."

"Well, that's that," Elizabeth said as they stepped away from the registration counter at Caesars Palace. "We just can't afford this place." She watched Jessica's expectant smile dissolve.

"I'm sorry, Liz," Scott said as they began to walk slowly through the marble-pillared lobby. "I kept blabbing about how reasonable the prices are in Vegas. I totally forgot about the holiday rush. I guess we shouldn't have expected to get a cut rate at the last minute, on the night before New Year's Eve."

"We'd better drive out of town and find a cheap motel somewhere past the city," Elizabeth said. She hated to admit it, but she felt as disappointed as Jessica looked. Still, somebody had to be practical.

"What about someplace else on the Strip?" Jessica suggested, leading the way to the door. "We could try the Riviera or the Dunes."

Elizabeth shook her head. "I don't think there's any point, Jess. For one thing, it's getting late. We don't have all night to try every hotel in town."

"But Liz, please—"

"Besides," Elizabeth continued. "I bet all the big hotels are in the same price range. We have to ration our money on this trip, and Scott's got a semester of med school to pay for."

"She's right, Jessica," Scott said gently. "At these rates, we'll never be able to afford two rooms between the three of us."

Jessica stopped walking so abruptly that Elizabeth crashed into her. "I've got it!" she cried. "I've got the perfect solution for how we can stay at Caesars and still save money!"

Elizabeth raised her eyebrows. "Even if gambling was a good solution, Jess, you're not old enough."

"That's not what I meant. We can't afford two rooms between us. But we can afford one."

"What good will that do?" Elizabeth asked. "We can't make Scott stay in the Jeep. And I don't think they'll let him curl up under a blackjack table."

"No, dummy! He can curl up in our room. It'll have two beds, won't it? You and I can share one, and Scott can have the other."

Scott shook his head. "That's very nice of you, Jessica, but I don't think—"

"No way, Jessica!" Elizabeth said firmly. "What would Mom and Dad say? What would Tom say?"

"They wouldn't say a thing, because we're not going to tell them about it," Jessica declared, tossing her golden hair. "Sometimes you just have to go with the flow, Liz. What's the big deal? We're all adults."

"Sometimes I wonder."

"You're always telling me I let my emotions get in the way of clear, logical decision making. Who's being illogical now?"

"Jessica, you know as well as I do that we can't share a room with Scott. It just wouldn't be right!" What she really meant was that it wouldn't be safe. Scott was a nice enough guy, but they had only known him for a few hours. Asleep, they would be too vulnerable. Of course, Elizabeth didn't want to say that in front of Scott.

Jessica began ticking off points on her fingers. "My plan is economical: We all get a place to sleep, for the price of one measly room. My plan is fast and convenient: We're already here. And my plan is a blast—um, I mean it's educational: It gives us the opportunity to sample the, uh, diverse culture and unique atmosphere of one of our nation's most famous cities."

"Good try, but it's not going to work, Jess. You know this is a bad idea."

"Why? It'll be like a slumber party."

Elizabeth dropped her voice to a whisper. "Jess, it's not safe! We don't know anything about him!"

"We'll take turns getting dressed in the bathroom," Jessica said happily, ignoring Elizabeth's real objection. "If I know you, you packed pajamas that look like something Grandma would wear. And my nightshirt covers up a lot more of

71

me than what I have on now. I swear, Liz, you are the world's most boring eighteen-year-old. You're just being unreasonable, as usual!"

"And you're just being irresponsible, as usual!"

"You sound like Dad."

"I'll take that as a compliment."

Scott threw up his hands. "Whoa, girls! This is obviously not in the cards for tonight. Liz is right, Jessica. You wouldn't want to do anything you'd have to hide from your parents."

Elizabeth rolled her eyes. "Oh, no. Jessica would never want to do anything she'd have to hide from Mom and Dad."

Jessica turned on her. "And what's that supposed to mean? I never keep anything really important from them."

"Jessica, you got *married* last semester and didn't tell them."

Jessica grimaced. "I was just waiting for the right time to break the news. And I let them know eventually—after it was annulled."

Scott broke the tension with a wide grin. "This sounds like a story I'd love to hear sometime."

"Later," Elizabeth said curtly.

"But right now, we have a choice to make," Scott said. "I won't share a room with you girls if it's going to make Elizabeth even the slightest bit uncomfortable."

Jessica's face melted from anger to hope. "Come on, Liz!"

Elizabeth sighed, sick and tired of feeling like the world's most boring eighteen-year-old. She considered the options.

Jessica was right—it would be cheapest and most convenient to stay at Caesars. And they all were tired and hungry; it would be nice to stop traveling for the night. But Tom had been worried about the twins riding in the same car with a strange man. Sleeping with him in the next bed seemed a hundred times more dangerous.

Still, she thought, *it's not like Scott jumped at the chance to spend the night with us.* Any guy who was enough of a gentleman to side with Elizabeth on this issue was obviously not the kind of guy to take advantage of two vulnerable teenagers.

On the other hand, Jessica and Scott had been looking more and more chummy all day. When it came to men, willpower was not Jessica's strong point. *And I'm not Jessica's baby-sitter,* Elizabeth decided.

"I don't know, Scott," she said slowly. "Maybe I'm being too cautious."

Jessica opened her mouth to speak, but Scott silenced her with a look.

"You definitely are not being too cautious, Liz," he said. He jumped ahead of the attendant to hold the door open for the girls. "You're being responsible. You shouldn't apologize for having good judgment."

"Maybe not. But as much as I hate to admit it,

Jessica's arguments actually make some sense."

"I still don't like it," Scott said. "It isn't right for a guy like me to take advantage of two beautiful young women who have been so kind."

Elizabeth shook her head. "You wouldn't be taking advantage, Scott. We'd be splitting the cost evenly, three ways."

"You mean half."

"No, I don't. There's two of us and only one of you. You shouldn't have to pay for half the hotel room."

"But I'm taking one of two beds. So my rightful share is one-half."

"Well, all right. But don't you dare try to pay for dinner."

Jessica's eyes twinkled under the gold lights lining the roof of the covered driveway. "I guess this means we're staying at Caesars!"

Elizabeth wasn't sure how it had happened. But somehow, she had agreed that Scott would share the twins' room. She shrugged and turned back to the door. Jessica was right. Sometimes you had to go with the flow.

"That shrimp cocktail was amazing," Jessica said two hours later, leaning against Scott as the three strolled around the Mirage's spectacular, glass-domed atrium. "It was a great idea to eat dinner here, instead of staying at Caesars."

"I thought you liked Caesars!" Elizabeth said,

walking a little too closely behind them. Jessica sighed. As much as she loved her sister, she would have preferred to be alone with Scott. Especially now that his arm was around her waist and his cheek was lightly brushing against her hair. And especially since Elizabeth seemed intent on barging into the conversation every time Jessica began to feel intimate.

On the other hand, Jessica thought ruefully, getting intimate was what had gotten her into trouble during her first semester at college. Her romance with and marriage to Mike McAllery had progressed at lightning speed, and she'd ended up wishing her sister were around to help her out. Maybe it wasn't a bad idea to have Elizabeth nearby.

"I love Caesars," Jessica averred, pulling her thoughts back to the present. "But we already explored it on the way to find our room. This way, we get to spend some time in two classy hotels instead of just one."

"Did you notice the front desk here?" Scott pointed out. "It's got aquariums full of little sharks!"

"That's to discourage customers from taking home the hotel's towels," Elizabeth explained to her sister.

"Really?" Jessica asked. Then she noticed an amused twinkle in her twin's eye. She scowled at Elizabeth. The Wakefields always said Jessica was the world's most gullible person; Elizabeth couldn't resist proving it now and then.

"Don't worry, Jessica," Scott said, pulling her closer. "I'll protect you from the sharks. And the tigers."

"Tigers? What tigers?" Elizabeth asked. She spoke lightly, but Jessica heard the sharpness in her voice. Elizabeth was clearly mad at her sister. It was obvious that she disapproved of Jessica's growing relationship with Scott.

Jessica was still uncertain of the relationship herself, though he certainly was gorgeous. But Elizabeth's disapproval helped make up her mind. She leaned in closer, until she could feel Scott's warm lips brush lightly against her ear. "I guess you're joking about the tigers," she said.

"Oh, no," Scott breathed into her ear. "They've got a show here that uses real white tigers."

Jessica wasn't afraid of the tigers, but she snuggled against Scott as if she were. He responded by holding her tighter, just as she had planned. Jessica glanced defiantly at her sister. "You look awfully tired, Elizabeth," she said sweetly.

"For some reason, I ended up having to drive most of the way here," Elizabeth reminded her.

"Maybe we should get back to Caesars so you can get some rest."

"Don't you mean so *we* can get some rest?"

"Yes, of course," Jessica replied quickly, trying

to think of a way to be alone with Scott. "It's been a long day." She smiled at him. "I'm dying to go to bed."

A half hour later, she lay on top of the blankets on the bed she and Elizabeth were to share. She listened carefully for a rush of water in the bathroom. "Come on, Scott!" she said in a low voice. "Liz is in the shower. Now's our chance to sneak away."

"I don't know if this is a good idea, Jess. I don't want Liz to worry about you. I mean, she was nice enough to let me share your room."

"So we'll leave her a note," Jessica said. She grabbed a sheet of Caesars stationery and scrawled, *Liz—Gone to get change for the soda machine. We'll be right back.*

Scott grinned. "You are downright devious. I like that in a woman." He plucked the Stetson hat from where it lay on the bed and placed it on Jessica's head. She smiled and followed him out of the room, her hand in his.

A few minutes later, they stopped to look at a secluded gazebo near one of the hotel's two swimming pools. The pool area was nearly deserted, and reflections from the full moon and the colored lights around them glinted on the surface of the water. Scott's arms were warm around her. The musky scent of his cologne was intoxicating. And in the moonlight, Jessica could almost make out her own face reflected in his mysterious gray eyes.

"Your hair is like starlight," he whispered into her ear, running his strong hand through her hair. He chuckled huskily. "I sound like a bad romance novel. But you are beautiful."

He traced the soft curve of her cheek, his fingers trailing fire wherever they touched her skin. Then he gently lifted her chin and kissed her with warm, insistent lips. Jessica responded greedily to his kiss. Her body tingled everywhere it touched his, as if the moonlight were pouring into her like liquid. She listened to the water lapping gently against the side of the pool, and she wished the kiss would never end.

Chapter Four

Scott's forehead was moist with sweat. He cursed himself silently; sweating in a climate-controlled room was bad form. That was for amateurs or low rollers—grinds, in Las Vegas parlance. Scott was no grind. And his first commandment of gambling was never to let the opposition see his anxiety. Nobody was supposed to know that his bankroll was down, that a single hour of late-night black-jack had cleaned him out. Nobody was supposed to know that the hundred-dollar chip he would bet on the next round was the last bit of money he had in the world.

Scott gazed steadily around him as the dealer shuffled the cards. The casino at Caesars was like Las Vegas itself. Extravagant and bustling, it exuded an almost disturbing combination of elegance and gaudiness. Marble pillars and a towering statue of Augustus Caesar competed for attention with rows of colorful slot machines and gaming tables.

Hundreds of well-dressed people dropped tokens into slots and laid bets on green felt-covered tables. But for all the activity, the room was strangely quiet. The inside of the casino was timeless; no clocks could be seen, and no clues from the outside world distracted gamblers from their betting. But Scott's wristwatch showed that it was after two in the morning. The people who were still on the floor at this hour were serious about their gambling.

The other two blackjack players were no different. A well-groomed woman of about fifty, in a white linen dress, had been playing well for the past hour. Now she took a turn cutting the cards for the pretty young dealer. The other player, a man in his mid-thirties, eyed her suspiciously. Scott scowled at him. The man was dressed as if he'd just come off a golf course—a bright blue golf shirt and plaid pants.

Scott scrutinized both players once more as the dealer began to lay down the cards. Like Scott, both had been betting the black chips that were worth a hundred dollars each, a sure sign of a serious game. Grinds used the five-dollar red chips most of the time, occasionally splurging with one of the green twenty-five-dollar chips. Scott had no patience for low rollers. *If you can't pull the trigger,* he always said, *stay away from the gun.* Risk was everything—it was the most exhilarating part of gambling.

But if this last risk didn't pay off, he could be left with nothing. Normally, he didn't take advantage of the free drinks casinos provided for gamblers—he liked to keep his wits about him. But he'd been losing for an hour, and his nerves were frazzled. A scotch on the rocks would calm him down, he'd reasoned. He was now on his third drink, and it wasn't working.

The dealer placed a card, facedown, in front of each player. First the golf pro, then the woman in white, Scott, and finally herself. But her fingers seemed to be moving in slow motion. *Get on with it!* Scott wanted to yell. *I have to know!* He bit his tongue and tried not to look nervous.

It was all Jessica's fault, he decided. Jessica, with the starlit hair and the winning smile. Oh, he didn't think he was exactly falling for her; she wasn't his type. But she had caught him off guard. She'd somehow managed to wheedle her way past his usual indifference. That bothered him. And now, the thought of her was making him lose his cool in an uncharacteristic way. And that was making him lose his money.

The deal was finished. Each player had two cards, facedown. The dealer's second card was showing. A nine of hearts.

"Damn," Scott whispered under his breath. *That could be hard to beat.* He slowly tilted up his own cards so that only he could see them.

A nine and a ten.

Not bad, he told himself. *But still no sure thing.* Scott stared at the dealer's card as if he could peer through its back. Like Scott, the dealer was "standing"—playing with what she had, rather than taking another card. She couldn't beat him unless her card was a ten or an ace.

The game flowed on in slow motion. Its outcome was crucial for Scott. If he won his money back, he could go on with his trip, as originally planned. If not, his options were limited.

The man in plaid and the woman in white each accepted a third card. Then came the moment of truth.

Plaid-pants scowled. His cards totaled twenty-three. The woman had eighteen. Scott flipped over his own cards—the nine and the ten—his eyes glued to the dealer's hand. He had nineteen. She turned over her card. *An ace.* That gave her twenty.

Scott watched stonily as his last hundred-dollar chip disappeared with those of the other players. He was broke now.

Dead broke.

"Scott, you look exhausted. Did you sleep okay?" Elizabeth asked the next morning as she packed her clothes. Scott sat on his bed and stared out the window, not saying a word.

"Scott?" she repeated. "Are you all right?"

"I'm fine!" he growled. Immediately he looked sheepish. "I'm sorry, Liz. I didn't mean to bite your head off. I guess I am kind of tired."

Jessica emerged from the bathroom looking as perfect as a fashion model. "Which of the restaurants are we going to try for breakfast? Will a T-shirt be dressy enough?" she asked. "I can change if you want to go to one of the fancier places."

"Don't change," Elizabeth ordered. "The coffee shop is all we can afford."

"To tell you the truth," Scott said, "I'm shorter on cash than I thought. Why don't we get a jump on driving now, before the traffic starts? We can go to the outskirts of town and then eat at a truck stop. It's bound to be cheaper, and we'll make better time."

Jessica looked like she was about to protest.

"Sounds good to me," Elizabeth said quickly, tucking her red blouse into her jeans. "Come on, Jess. Are you all packed?"

"I'm coming; keep your shirt on," Jessica retorted. Then she turned to Scott. "That doesn't go for you, of course," she added with a mischievous grin. Scott grinned back, but Elizabeth thought he looked a little nervous. *Maybe he's starting to realize he's in over his head with Jessica,* she thought.

"Watch what you answer, Scott," she warned

him. "Jessica can be pretty dangerous to a nice guy like yourself."

Scott's gray eyes didn't leave Jessica's face. "I can be pretty dangerous myself," he said. His smile was guileless, but something in his voice troubled Elizabeth. She wished he had chosen any other word. *Dangerous* attracted Jessica the way flame attracted a moth.

Tom's warnings about Scott played back in Elizabeth's mind, but she shoved them away. *I'm just worried because Jessica has fallen so quickly for this guy,* she told herself. *I don't want to see her hurt again.*

"Gross," Jessica said as she finished the last of her coffee. "That trucker at the counter is being disgusting again." Vulgar, overweight truckers were not something Jessica wanted to look at first thing in the morning—or anytime, for that matter.

Scott's mouth was set in a grim line. "What's he doing now?"

"Just leering at me, like before," Jessica said. She was glad Scott was with her to keep men like that from coming too close.

She flashed Scott a private smile. The kiss last night had changed everything. Yesterday, she had been wildly infatuated. Now, she realized, she was feeling something much deeper. She couldn't stay away from him. She could hardly even look away from him. There was a magnetism about him that she couldn't resist.

"I'm glad the jerk is sitting too far away to make any more rude remarks," Elizabeth commented. "You'd think these guys would get it—in the whole history of the automobile, I bet no trucker has ever managed to pick up girls by saying things like, 'Ooh, blondie, you've got my motor running.'"

The heavyset trucker stood up and tossed a bill on the counter. Then he slapped a baseball cap onto his head and turned to leer at the twins once more. He licked his lips and strutted out of the diner.

Jessica made a face. "How totally sickening! And he wasn't even good looking." Then she noticed that Scott was standing with his fists clenched, his gray eyes narrowed as he stared after the trucker. "Hey, Scott, chill out. It's sweet of you to want to defend us, but we're fine."

Elizabeth glanced at her watch. "We should get going. It's past seven thirty."

Jessica rolled her eyes. "Your wish is our command, Miss Punctuality."

Elizabeth paid the check and they stepped into the white glare of early-morning sunlight. As they headed for the Jeep, Jessica noticed the trucker standing a few feet away. He was still ogling them. Jessica rolled her eyes, and Scott stepped in front of the twins.

"Now ain't that a sight?" the trucker said, tipping the brim of his cap. "Double the fun—hey, boy?"

Elizabeth scowled and opened the driver's-side door of the Jeep. "Get lost!" she said to the trucker. "Jessica, get in. Now."

Jessica stood still. Her gaze shifted from the leering trucker to Scott, whose fists were clenched so hard that his knuckles were turning white.

"You are two of the prettiest little blondes ever to hit Nevada," the trucker continued. "So, buddy, the packaging sure looks real good, but are they as sweet on the inside?"

Scott let loose. With a strangled cry, he jumped forward and landed a brutal punch in the trucker's ample midsection. The older man crumpled to his knees, clutching his stomach. Scott cuffed him across the face. Blood ran from the trucker's nose.

"Jessica," Scott said in a quiet voice. "Get in the Jeep."

Jessica complied silently, shaken by the coldness on Scott's handsome face.

A minute later, the Jeep was speeding northeast on I-15. "You didn't have to hit that man," Elizabeth said to Scott, who was sitting beside her in the front. "He probably wouldn't have hurt us. We could have just walked away."

"I didn't mean to upset you," Scott said. "But I know his type. He might have followed through on some of that garbage he was spouting."

"And he might not have!"

"Yes, but we have no way of knowing that," Scott answered, a little calmer. "I didn't want to take any chances with you girls. I didn't really hurt him. I just let him know that the two of you are off limits."

Jessica took a deep breath. As frightening as the incident had been, everyone was fine. The trucker would be back on his feet, propositioning truck-stop waitresses in half an hour. Besides, it was really kind of romantic, having a great-looking guy fight for her. "He was only trying to help, Liz."

Scott sighed. "I'm sorry, ladies." He smiled sheepishly. The cruelty had vanished from his handsome features, and he looked like his old self again. "I guess I was out of control. I shouldn't have lost my temper like that."

"It's no big deal," Jessica assured him. "Anyway, it's over now."

Scott shook his head. "Maybe, but Elizabeth is absolutely right. Violence never solves anything. Forgive me, Liz?"

Elizabeth nodded, her face still pale. "Yes, of course," she breathed. "Jessica's right. It's over."

An hour later, Elizabeth pulled the Jeep into the parking lot of a convenience store near the Moapa Indian reservation. After Jessica's record root-beer consumption of the day before,

Elizabeth had meant to keep their pit stops today to a minimum. But this one couldn't be helped.

"Why are we stopping?" Scott asked quickly.

Elizabeth shrugged. "I need to use the bathroom and the phone," she said apologetically. "I told Tom I'd call to let him know we got started in plenty of time. If you two want to grab some food for the road, now's your chance."

Scott nodded, slipping on a jean jacket and rifling through his duffel bag. "Good idea. I do need to stock up on a few things." He hoisted the bag as Elizabeth spotted the phone booth, which was just outside the door of the bright, modern store. "No need for you to come in, Jess," Elizabeth heard him say as she started toward the phone. "You wait in the Jeep, and I'll bring you whatever you want."

"Chocolate-chip cookies," Jessica replied instantly. "And something low fat for Elizabeth."

Jessica watched as Scott sauntered across the parking lot, swinging that duffel bag he seemed to carry everywhere he went. *What a body!* she thought again. She closed her eyes and leaned back in the seat, remembering the touch of his lips on hers, the smell of his cologne, and the shimmering play of lights on the surface of the water. *That had to be the most romantic moment of my entire life.* On impulse, Jessica threw on the cowboy hat Scott had left on the backseat. She leaped out of the car and ran to catch up with him.

She grabbed his arm just outside the door of the shop. Scott jumped as if he'd been attacked.

"What the hell are you doing? I told you to wait in the car!"

"What's the big deal? I want to come in with you."

"Dammit, Jessica. Do as you're told!"

Ignoring him, Jessica pushed open the door and stepped inside. She scanned the interior. No other customers were shopping at this early hour. Behind the counter, an exotic-looking young woman was fitting a paper filter into a coffeepot.

All at once, Jessica was acutely aware of Scott standing directly behind her, his body very close to hers. *He certainly is moody today,* she thought. One minute he was pushing her away, and the next he was practically melting into her back. Not that she objected. For an instant, Scott's hand brushed against her waist. She thought she felt something hard and cold through her thin T-shirt.

Jessica froze. Scott's hand was thrust in front of her. And it was holding a gun.

"This is a stickup!" Scott yelled. "Move back from that counter with your hands in the air!"

Jessica jumped as the gun exploded, very close

to her. She was looking at the store's surveillance camera as it shattered into shards of glass and metal.

"Everything's fine, Tom," Elizabeth said. "We got an early start like I'd planned. We were out of Vegas before seven o'clock. This is a really lousy connection."

"It sure is," he agreed, his deep voice thin and riddled with static. "Maybe I should try to call you back."

"Don't bother," Elizabeth said. "I can't talk long."

"Where are you?" he asked. "Is that Scott guy still with you?"

"Yes, he is. But don't worry. We'll be in Vail in time for the party tonight—" She jumped at a loud burst of noise from somewhere nearby.

"Liz, what was that?" crackled Tom's voice.

"I—I don't know," she stammered. From inside the phone booth, she couldn't even tell where the sound had come from. She choked down a rush of fear. "It must have been a car backfiring. I'm close to the road here—"

Several more sharp explosions rang out in quick succession. Elizabeth gasped. *Oh, my God, was that Jessica screaming?*

A moment later Scott ran from the building, pushing a sobbing Jessica in front of him. There was blood on her face. Scott reached into the phone booth, grabbed the receiver, and slammed it down.

"Get in the Jeep, now!" he yelled.

Only then did Elizabeth notice the revolver in his hand.

Chapter Five

Tom stood in his dorm room, gripping the phone in his hand.

"Elizabeth!" he yelled into the receiver once more. But he knew he'd hear only silence. The line was dead.

What had made those noises? Had a car backfired on the highway, or was that gunshots? It sounded like gunshots. But he couldn't be sure through the static on the line.

There had been a click, and then nothing. Had the line gone dead because of a problem in the phone system? Or had Elizabeth—or somebody else—hung up on him?

He considered calling the police. But he had nothing to tell them. Elizabeth hadn't mentioned her location. He wasn't even sure she was still in Nevada; she could easily be in Utah by now. A few sharp pops and a vague sense of dread weren't exactly evidence that his girlfriend and her sister were in trouble.

He dropped the receiver back onto its hook. If the line had simply gone dead, Elizabeth would call him back in a minute. They would laugh over his crazy fears, and then he would go on packing for his noon flight to Denver. But maybe she wouldn't call. Maybe the line went dead because it was out of order. Or maybe Elizabeth wouldn't bother trying to get back to him, figuring she'd already let him know her timetable for the day.

But what if something terrible had happened? What if Elizabeth and Jessica were caught in the middle of one of those armed robberies the police were investigating?

Tom shook his head and tried to rein in his imagination. He returned to packing. But he kept watching the silent telephone, desperately wishing it would ring.

Scott yanked Elizabeth out of the phone booth and pulled her toward the Jeep, still pushing Jessica in front of him. Elizabeth cringed every time she saw the cold-looking steel of the gun touch Jessica's back.

"Get in!" he commanded both girls, waving the gun at Elizabeth. "Drive, Liz—fast! Stop bawling, Jessica." He climbed into the backseat with Jessica, but he kept the gun trained on Elizabeth.

"You shot her!" Jessica said through her tears. "Did you have to shoot her?"

"Dammit, Jess. I told you not to follow me in there. I didn't want you involved in any of this." Elizabeth shuddered when she caught sight of his face in the rearview mirror. An odd, triumphant gleam lit his eyes. "Faster, Elizabeth!" he barked.

Elizabeth's hands trembled as she steered the Jeep down the interstate. Her heart was beating so loudly, she was sure Scott could hear it from the backseat. "Are you all right, Jessica?" she asked, her voice coming out as a squeak. "Is that blood on your face?"

Jessica wiped her cheek with her sleeve. "It's only a tiny cut," she said, still sobbing, "from a piece of glass."

A few minutes later, Elizabeth heard a whining sound in the distance. Sirens. She took a deep breath. Maybe the police were on their trail. Maybe she and Jessica would be rescued, unharmed. The sirens grew louder. Her heart flip-flopped between terror and relief.

Miraculously, Scott seemed calmer now, almost as if he were enjoying himself. The thought of it made her angry.

"You seem to be in your element," she said darkly, trying to keep her voice from wavering. "This is quite a hobby for an ear-nose-and-throat man. A doctor like you would have plenty of patients."

Scott pushed the gun against her shoulder. "Don't make this any worse, Liz," he said evenly. "Just keep quiet and do what I say, and nobody will get hurt."

Elizabeth nodded, too numb to speak. As the Jeep topped a low rise in the road, she saw the flashing light of a police car emerge over a swell in the distance behind them. The area around them seemed mostly flat, with mountains on the horizon. But the landscape undulated with low hills and valleys that were almost invisible until you came upon them. The chasing police car seemed to be crawling along the highway at a maddeningly slow pace. A moment later, it disappeared into a valley in the road.

The gun jabbed at Elizabeth's shoulder. "There's a right turn just ahead," Scott said. "Take it. Don't slow down. Go a mile and then make a sharp left onto the gravel road." Elizabeth glanced into the rearview mirror, hoping to catch another glimpse of the pursuing police car. *Dammit, I said turn!*

Elizabeth choked back a sob.

Scott took a deep breath as she turned onto the secondary road. "I'm sorry, Liz. And you too, Jess. I didn't mean to scare you. But there's a lot going on here that you don't know anything about. I don't want to hurt either of you. All I want is a ride to safety. Just do exactly as I say and we'll all get out of this fine. Trust me."

"Trust you?" Jessica sputtered. Elizabeth glanced back at her sister. Jessica was hunched against the side of the Jeep, as far away from Scott as possible in the cramped backseat. Her white-knuckled fingers nervously twisted the hem of her SVU T-shirt. "I don't understand any of this," she whispered. "Scott, you shot that woman back there!"

"Don't worry about her, Jessica. I know just where to aim so she'll be okay." Jessica seemed a little relieved, but Elizabeth didn't believe him for an instant. "You know I'm not a killer."

"I don't know anything about you," Jessica replied. "Why are you doing this?"

Elizabeth pursed her lips and shook her head at her twin. Through her cotton blouse, the gun felt cold against her shoulder. Now was not the time to ask questions.

Scott peered into the rearview mirror, careful to keep his Colt .45 steady against Elizabeth's shoulder. He breathed a sigh of relief. The police hadn't followed him off the interstate. By the time they realized he'd eluded them, he'd be almost to the state line.

"This wasn't the way I planned things," he told the girls. *That's an understatement,* he thought. When he accepted the ride in the Jeep the day before, Scott had decided to leave the twins out of his little shopping trips completely.

He had managed to rob the gas station near the state border while Elizabeth talked with Tom. But he hadn't fired a shot. A crack on the back of the head with a .357 Magnum had downed the clerk, permanently. Scott was no med student, but he knew plenty about head injuries.

But the clerk near the border was supposed to be the only casualty. He hadn't wanted any more of that kind of action until he was traveling alone again. Squeaky-clean Jessica and Elizabeth would fit into his line of work about as well as he'd fit in at medical school. "Partners, I don't need," he muttered.

"Then let us go!" Elizabeth said in her quiet, intense voice. "Take the Jeep, but let us off by the side of the road."

Scott shook his head. "I'm afraid I can't do that. For now, at least, we're all in this together."

A siren became audible in the distance and then faded out again.

"Damn," Scott said under his breath. "How did I get myself into this?"

The situation had begun to sour the night before, at the blackjack table. When he realized he was broke, he knew he had to take a risk and rob one more store, even if he couldn't choose it as carefully as he normally would have. Scott didn't mind risk. But today he'd botched everything.

It wasn't just allowing Jessica to follow him

into the convenience store. "I didn't count on a surveillance camera," he said aloud.

"And we didn't count on any of this!" Elizabeth said. Tears were running down her cheeks, but she was struggling to regain control of her emotions.

Scott turned his thoughts back to the surveillance camera. Most of the time, he chose targets that were strictly low tech. Oh, he'd occasionally hit places with silent alarms, but he always cased them carefully. He always knew just what to expect and how to act to keep anyone from getting suspicious. Losing all his money last night had made him desperate. And desperate men got careless.

Of course, he'd shot the surveillance camera out as soon as he'd noticed it. But for the first time, the police might have his face on film. He fought back a feeling of dread. *Why the heck didn't I wear that bandanna?* he asked himself. But he knew the answer. He hadn't wanted to tip off the twins that he wasn't exactly what he appeared to be—a medical student on his way to Vail.

Now, even with his picture on a videotape, he was sure he could still escape if he got out of the state fast.

"Where are we going?" Elizabeth asked in a controlled voice.

"Just drive!" he barked. But the question was a good one. Where would he go?

The twins had been heading toward the Utah

border. But Utah was too risky for Scott. The cops there had begun tracking him. He sensed it, the same way he'd sensed for the last few days that somebody in Nevada was on his trail. He scanned the detailed, internal map of the West that he kept locked in his mind. He had lied to Elizabeth about being bad with directions. Scott always knew exactly where he was going.

The California line was in the wrong direction. His best bet now was Mexico. And the quickest route ran through Arizona. The police had been following the twins' Jeep, but they hadn't been close enough to get a good look. They couldn't know the license plate number, and they couldn't know that it belonged to the Wakefield twins. That meant he was safe for a while. He'd use the girls and their Jeep to get into Arizona—whether they liked it or not.

When it came down to it, he decided, protecting himself was more important than protecting the twins. He was sorry to expose them to danger. But that was the price they paid for picking up strange men.

If he had won last night's blackjack game, things would be different. He'd have options for getting to Mexico. He would have found an excuse to ditch the twins. Then he could grab a bus or hitch a ride with a trucker.

Instead, the Wakefield twins were involved in all of it—involved right up to their pretty little identical blond heads. And in another few hours, they would have to lose those heads. Scott's policy was to take care of witnesses.

He glanced at Jessica, huddled in the corner, her eyes wide with fear. Part of him would be sorry to kill her. She was a nice kid, even if she did talk incessantly. She didn't look as if she could choke out a sentence right now to save her life. Of course, nothing could save her life anymore. She knew who Scott was. She and Elizabeth could identify him. They had to die.

It was Scott's only chance for escape.

"The surveillance tape from this morning's holdup is here," Keisha Williamson said, poking her head into the doorway of Jeff's office. "They didn't have a setup for audio, but they say the few seconds of video they've got are pretty clear."

Jeff followed her toward the viewing room. "I still can't believe the Moapa police report about the suspect. Have you seen the tape?"

"Of course I haven't seen it," she shot back. "Would I risk the wrath of Jeff Marks by not letting you know the instant it arrived? You've been on the rampage all morning—I wasn't even about to open the package without you present."

Jeff opened his mouth to apologize. But a video technician, Fran Peters, handed him the tape, and everything else fled his mind. He stared at the tape in his hand, unable to move. So far, the police report sounded almost like the others. It was a small store just off the interstate. It took place early in the morning, at a time when there weren't many people driving by. And the one clerk—a young Paiute woman from the nearby reservation—was in a coma and not expected to live. Jeff might not be able to prove a connection to the other incidents throughout Nevada and Utah. But he could get the suspect for armed robbery, assault with a deadly weapon, and attempted murder. If the clerk died, the charge was first-degree murder.

For the first time, Jeff felt he really had a chance of bringing in a suspect. The video made all the difference. He would finally see the robber's face on tape. Jeff turned impatiently to Fran, who had taken the courier's package from him and was fitting the tape into the television set. Several agents filed into the room to watch.

"Here you are, Jeffrey," Fran said, pushing the play button. "It's show time."

Jeff stared at the screen. The video camera panned the deserted store—clean and well kept— with a black-haired woman in her early twenties making a pot of coffee behind the counter. Jeff's throat tightened at the sight of her—another beautiful woman about to become a victim. Just like Summer.

"It's a little dark," Keisha complained. "Can you brighten up the picture any?"

Fran fiddled with the controls. "No. It must have been taken early in the morning, and the windows don't let in much light."

As Jeff watched breathlessly, the door of the shop opened and the suspect walked in. For a moment, the figure was in shadow. All Jeff could tell was that the person wore a light-colored Stetson. Then the figure stepped under a fluorescent light, and Jeff gasped. "This can't be right! Are you sure this is the correct tape?"

"Positive," Keisha told him. A gun flashed on the screen, and the picture went black.

"I'll rewind it and show you again," Fran offered.

Jeff watched it through once more, as if he expected the suspect to change this time, to fit his expectations. Then he shook his head. "Well, I guess tapes don't lie." His suspect—the person who had shot the store clerk and who might have killed Summer—looked about eighteen years old. And it was a clean-cut, pretty girl, with long, blond hair and an open, innocent face.

"I'm sorry, Liz," Jessica said in a quiet voice as the Jeep bounced over a gravel road somewhere near Lake Mead. "You said we shouldn't pick up a guy we didn't know. But I wouldn't listen to you. This is all my fault."

"Jessica, it's not anybody's fault," Scott told

her. "But you should have stayed in the Jeep back there, like I told you to."

Jessica ignored him. "How could I be so stupid?" she said to her sister. "You were trying to be practical, but I wouldn't let you."

"Jess, it won't do any good to blame yourself now," Elizabeth said. Jessica could hear the strain in her voice. "Besides, I knew it was risky, and I agreed anyhow. It's just as much my fault as yours."

"Do you have to hold the gun on her like that?" Jessica asked, close to panic. "She's driving, just like you told her to! All you're doing is making things harder for her." She breathed a sigh of relief as Scott lowered the gun from Elizabeth's shoulder. But then he turned it on Jessica instead. She stifled a scream.

"I told you, I don't want to hurt either one of you," Scott reminded her. "But I will if either of you screws up my plans."

"You and Steven are right, Liz. I'm a crummy judge of character—especially when it comes to guys."

Elizabeth glared at Scott. "No argument here."

"I'll make it up to you, Lizzie. I promise I will."

"Jessica, that's not—"

"I mean it!" Jessica vowed tearfully. "If we get out of this, I'll be more responsible like you. I'll be—"

Scott pushed the gun against the side of her head. "Cut it out, Jessica! Now both of you be quiet and just drive. Elizabeth, you'll cross a bridge just up ahead. Then take the dirt road to the left. It's a shortcut."

"A shortcut to where?" Elizabeth asked.

"None of your business," he growled. He lowered the gun so that it was pointing at Jessica's collarbone, which was less scary than having it touching her temple—but only a little less. Scott was beginning to sound angry again.

Jessica looked at the grim line of her sister's mouth in the rearview mirror. Elizabeth was as tense as she'd ever seen her. *And it's all my fault for being so irresponsible,* Jessica thought. *Well, I'm going to get us both out of this,* she decided solemnly, staring at the gleaming revolver. *I'm going to find a way to escape.*

"We're not going to let her escape this time," Jeff vowed to the other agents. Fran handed him a print that she'd made from the surveillance tape. He scrutinized the photo of the beautiful blond teenager in the Stetson hat, before holding it up for the other agents to see.

Something disturbed Jeff about the girl's face—something about her looked vaguely familiar, he realized. He filed the thought away for future reference. Maybe she had a police record. He might have seen her mug shot somewhere.

"Hey, what's that on her T-shirt?" asked Keisha. "It looks like an insignia from a school."

"Sweet Valley University," one of the other agents read. "I think it's in Southern California."

"Then that's where you'll start, Keisha," Jeff said. "I want you to take a copy of this print with you."

"You want me to go to Sweet Valley University?" Keisha asked.

"That's right. Try the admissions office, sorority houses, student newspapers, yearbooks—"

Keisha shook her head. "No, not yearbooks," she decided. "I doubt she's in any yet. My guess is that she's a freshman. At the most, she looks about eighteen."

Jeff shrugged. "Maybe there's some kind of freshman class directory. I don't know—see what you can find. But I want that girl's name!"

Keisha nodded. "Sure, Jeff. But a lot of people wear college T-shirts. She might not even be a student there."

"I know. And it's a good bet she's not. A female college student doesn't exactly fit the profile for armed robbery."

"Maybe she's a recent dropout," another agent suggested. "Or maybe she got the shirt from a relative who goes to school there."

"Anything's possible," Jeff admitted. "Anyway, we don't have a lot else to go on. So get yourself to Sweet Valley, California, and see what you can turn up."

Keisha shrugged. "You're the boss. It's funny, though—she sure doesn't look like a killer."

Fran shook her head. "No, she doesn't. In fact, she looks petrified, if you ask me—not exactly the expression of a callous murderer."

"I thought I knew who I was looking for," Jeff said. "I had the guy all figured out. But obviously I didn't know what I was talking about!"

"It's not over until it's over," Keisha said. "Who knows what we might turn up?"

Jeff shook his head. "As I said before, tapes don't lie. And we can't take any chances with this girl, pretty or not. The suspect should be considered armed and dangerous.

"I'll need somebody to coordinate for me here at HQ," Jeff said brusquely, pointing to one agent. "You'll be synthesizing reports from the field and from Washington and passing on to me any information that seems relevant. What are we still waiting for, Keisha?"

Keisha consulted a clipboard. "There's a lot of outstanding data on this one, Jeff. For one thing, we don't have the forensic report from that Paiute clerk this morning. It should be in this afternoon."

Jeff nodded. "And the folks in D.C. are running a computer search for that old blue or gray sedan that keeps turning up—if it really is the same sedan in every case."

"Can we really expect much from that search, without a license plate number?" somebody asked.

"Probably not," Jeff said, feeling overwhelmed by the amount of evidence he didn't have.

"The police in four states are on alert," Keisha said, obviously trying to cheer him up. "If we're lucky, they'll call in with something new. Where will you be, Jeff?"

"I'm going to nose around Moapa to see what the local cops have missed. I'll be setting up a field office in the vicinity. Fran, I'll want you with me. Have somebody find us a space." He crossed the room to a map on which he had marked every robbery site.

"Where do you want us to concentrate our roadblocks?" asked an older agent.

"I think she's heading for California," Jeff said. "Focus your attention there. Nobody gets past that state line without being stopped—and I mean nobody!"

"I'll coordinate with the state police on both sides of the border. But what makes you think she'll try to leave Nevada?"

"Our girl's been crisscrossing the state from top to bottom," Jeff explained, pointing to the map. "Now she's near the southern tip. She must know we're on her trail. So she'll try to make a run for it."

"How do you know she'll go to California?"

"I don't," Jeff replied. "But look at the map. I-15 is the only major artery in the region. From Moapa, she could head either northeast into Arizona and Utah, or southwest through Vegas and into California."

Keisha nodded. "I guess we can count Utah out. If you're right, and she's already hit seven stores in Utah, she won't risk going back there."

Jeff nodded. "California's another story. There's a lot of secondary roads along the California border between Vegas and Death Valley. I want them all covered."

The phone rang as he was speaking. He motioned to Keisha to pick it up. Meanwhile, the older agent crossed his arms and examined the map. "What about Arizona?"

"Set up a roadblock on the highway, at the state line," Jeff directed. "There aren't many other places she can cross into Arizona."

"I see what you mean. She can't get over Lake Mead without somebody seeing her; she won't take that chance. The only other spot is along this stretch north of the lake. What do you know about that area?"

"The terrain's rugged—it's the Valley of Fire region. There aren't a lot of roads, and most of those are lousy. A person would have to know the landscape pretty darn well in order to negotiate them. Cover that area as best you can. But if she keeps up the pattern she's established, she'll be heading toward California."

Keisha hung up the phone. "Jeff, we may have something here. The state police spotted a black Jeep that was speeding on I-15 outside of Moapa. They think it turned off on the route to Lake Mead, but they lost it there."

"Any connection to the shooting?"

"Nothing definite, but somebody saw a black Jeep in the parking lot of the store at about the time of the robbery."

"Sounds as definite as anything else we've got," Jeff said. He turned back to the map. "Though I don't know how it ties in with the blue or gray sedan."

"If she's traveling off road," the gray-haired agent reminded him, "then there's not much way we can catch her in that country."

Jeff nodded. "I know. Let's stick to the interstates for now. She's got to come out on one eventually. All right, get to it, everyone. You have your assignments."

Jeff walked back to his office, lost in thought. He couldn't believe how wrong he'd been in his own assessment of the armed robber. Was he losing his touch? Maybe everyone who had tried to warn him off this case was right. Maybe he was too close to it to be effective. But it was because of Summer that he was determined to solve the case.

Still, something seemed wrong. Every instinct

in his body told him the beautiful blond girl in the Stetson was not his perpetrator. He had a feeling there was more to the story than the video revealed. He stared at the print of his suspect. Again, something in the girl's big, frightened eyes sparked a reaction in Jeff. He couldn't believe that this innocent-looking girl had shot his fiancée in cold blood.

He picked up Summer's photograph and cradled it in his hands. Slowly starting to relax, he closed his eyes and recalled her sunny smile and her laughing blue eyes. But another image rushed in and replaced them—the image of Summer's bullet-riddled body at the morgue. Rage and anguish roiled inside Jeff. The blonde's innocent look and frightened eyes must be a facade. The video made it clear that she was a murderer.

Her eyes. That was it.

Jeff's armed-robbery suspect had the same blue-green eyes as his murdered fiancée. For a moment, he was gripped with horror. It seemed obscene, that a murderer and her victim should have the same lovely eyes.

Jeff took a deep breath. Then he slammed a clip of ammunition into his nine-millimeter pistol, shoved the gun into his shoulder holster, and headed out the door. "I will find that girl," he vowed in a whisper. "And I will bring her to justice—dead or alive."

Chapter Six

Scott scanned the rocky terrain for a dirt road he knew was somewhere close by. As the Jeep passed, a large bird rose from a ledge near the road and circled upward in long, lazy spirals. It looked like a bald eagle. He noticed that Jessica's eyes were fastened on it.

"We're going to be turning right in another half-mile or so," he told Elizabeth. "Then we'll go about a mile to a slightly bigger road where there's a gas station."

"Whatever you say," Elizabeth stammered, glancing back at the revolver he now held to her right shoulder. "But we don't really need it. The tank's nowhere near empty."

"I know. But we'll be getting into some countryside that's pretty remote." *It had better be remote*, he told himself. *I don't want anyone to find the twins' bodies until I'm hell and gone from here.*

But to Elizabeth, he said only, "I don't want to be caught in the middle of nowhere with an empty gas tank."

Another thing he didn't mention to Elizabeth was that it was safer to stop soon—before every rinky-dink sheriff's office in the state had his photograph up on its bulletin board. With his picture on tape somewhere, he would have to be a lot more careful.

"As long as we're stopping, Scott," Jessica began in a small, scared voice, "I really need to use the bathroom."

Scott looked at her tearstained face and huge eyes. "All right," he agreed. "The place I'm thinking of is just up ahead."

Elizabeth pulled the Jeep into the parking lot of the small country service station. "I guess I have to go, too."

Scott nodded. "Okay. But park the Jeep at the pump on this side of the lot, where it can't be seen from the windows of the building. Now, both of you—take a look at the door of the ladies' room. See where that's located? From out here, and even from inside the station, I'll have a clear view of that door. So don't bother trying to make a run for it."

"We won't," Jessica said in a resigned voice—a little too resigned, Scott thought.

"Even when you can't see my gun," he warned her, "remember that it's right here under my

114

jacket. And I can shoot faster than you can run. Besides, there's nowhere to run to out here." He gestured around the rugged landscape. The road twisted among ridges of sandstone banded in scarlet. The land was rocky, barren, and inhospitable. If not for the sun-splashed colors of the sand and rock, Scott could have imagined himself on the surface of the moon. Two California girls with no water and no gear couldn't hope to survive long in this terrain.

Jessica and Elizabeth nodded and walked slowly toward the bathroom, hand in hand. Scott tipped his hat to them, as if the three were still happy traveling companions on a fun-filled road trip to Vail. Way overhead, the eagle, still circling, tipped a wing, as if in response. Scott kept his eyes on the door of the ladies' room as he filled the Jeep's tank. Jessica had looked scared, all right. But he had also seen a look of grim resolve in those blue-green eyes of hers. Scott had a feeling that Jessica was up to something.

Jeff sat in the temporary field office that was being set up around him, near Moapa. The office was really a vacant storefront along the highway west of town. He stood near the only piece of furniture already in place—a dented metal desk that looked like a castoff. Two men were carrying in another metal desk, which was equally beat up. *As usual, the Bureau spares no expense for the Nevada*

115

office, he thought. But a telephone, a computer, and a fax machine were set up in front of him, next to Summer's photograph. And all three seemed to be in working order.

He gulped some scalding coffee. Then he picked up the phone and asked long-distance information for the number of the newspaper office in Sweet Valley, California. He'd already circulated the suspect's photograph to every police department within a five-hundred-mile radius. But sometimes answers came faster through unofficial channels.

Small-town newspapers heard the letters *F-B-I* and saw visions of Pulitzers. He couldn't use such information without official verification, of course. But sometimes it was the best place to start, especially since every other inquiry seemed to lead to a dead end.

Jeff leaned on the desk, wishing the movers would bring in a chair. He stared longingly into Summer's blue-green eyes. Then he looked at the photograph of his armed-robbery suspect. How could two such beautiful women be so frighteningly different?

His thoughts were interrupted by the frenzied voice of the editor at the *Sweet Valley News.* He put Summer out of his mind.

"I'm trying to locate a young woman who's wanted for questioning out here," he explained after identifying himself. "We have reason to believe she's from the Sweet Valley area."

"What can I do for you?" the woman asked uncertainly.

"It would be a big help if you'd let me fax you a copy of her picture, to see if you can get me a name and address for her."

"I don't know how much help I can be," the editor admitted. "We don't have a computerized system for matching a photograph, and we're awfully short-staffed, with the holidays and all. . . ."

Jeff didn't have a background in psychology for nothing. There was one sure way to motivate a newspaper editor. "I have to ask that you refrain from printing a story until we have something definite," he explained. "But as soon as we have a positive identification of the suspect and are ready to press charges, I would be happy to cooperate fully in an interview for any article you plan to write."

He could practically hear her panting. FBI agents were notoriously closemouthed about their cases. Jeff knew that a promise of an interview was more precious than gold to an editor. "I can't guarantee anything," she told him. "But fax the photograph to me, and I'll see what I can do."

A minute later, the photograph of the pretty blonde was sliding into Jeff's fax machine and spurting out of a machine at the *Sweet Valley News*, more than three hundred miles away.

"You're not going to believe this," came her

surprised voice through the receiver. "But I recognize this girl."

Jeff choked on his coffee. "You're kidding! Has she been arrested for armed robbery there?"

"No, that's not it," the editor said. "I don't remember who she is or why she was in the news. But I know we've run a picture of this woman before—a big photo, on page one. It was a couple years ago, maybe."

Jeff forced himself to breathe. "Can you remember anything at all about the woman? What about the story that ran with the photo?"

"That's a hard one. As I said, it was years ago. It was something tragic, I remember. . . . Oh, I know! It had something to do with the death of a teenage boy."

A murder? Jeff wondered. This was beginning to sound promising. Maybe the blonde in the Stetson hat wasn't as innocent as she appeared.

"Here it is!" the editor cried. "I've got the file in front of me."

"Is there a photograph?"

"Just as I remembered—it's a big color photo on the front page. And it sure looks like your girl. I'll fax this to you in a sec."

"What does it say about her? Was she ever convicted?"

"According to this article, she was sixteen years old and was driving a car—a Jeep Wrangler—

home from a school dance. There was an accident, and a boy was killed."

"Are you sure it was an accident?"

"That's what the police decided at the time," the editor said. "And it wasn't your girl's fault; another driver turned himself in later. It was a hit-and-run."

Jeff felt let down; it wasn't exactly a dramatic criminal record. "What else can you tell me about her?"

"The article calls her a straight-A student. I think her father is a prominent attorney in town."

Jeff frowned. Again, his suspect didn't sound like a ruthless murderer. "What's her name?" he asked.

"Wakefield," the editor said. "Elizabeth Wakefield."

"Elizabeth!" Jessica said in an excited whisper, pointing to a small, high window in the rest room. It was the only way out. "This is it!" she screeched. "This is our chance to escape!"

Elizabeth bit her lip. "I don't know, Jessica. What if Scott sees us?"

"He's not going to see us. Look—Scott's got a clear view of this door. But the window's on the back of the building. As long as we stay behind the station, we can run pretty far without him seeing us."

"Run where? Scott was right. We're miles from

the nearest town. We're not dressed for a cold night, and we don't have food or water."

"We don't need them. We can hide in those ledges we saw until Scott gives up and drives away. Then we can run back here and get help from the people in the gas station." Unexpectedly, Jessica felt a deep pain, as if she'd been stabbed in the heart, when she thought of running away from Scott. *Get a clue!* she screamed to her disobedient heart. *So he's cute. He's still a total scumbag who pulled a gun on us! And he's probably going to kill us if we stick around.*

Jessica pushed away all thoughts of one perfect kiss by the pool. Her heart might not know any better, but her brain was convinced that she and Elizabeth had to get away. She stared intently at her sister.

"Liz, it's my fault we're in trouble—I never should have begged you to pick up a guy we didn't know. Let me get us out of this. Climb out the window and escape with me. Besides, I saw what he did to that woman."

Elizabeth was still shaking her head.

"Elizabeth, we're witnesses!" Jessica cried desperately. "What if he's planning to do the same thing to us? Did you think of that?"

Elizabeth grimaced. "I haven't been able to think of anything else for the last hour." She sighed. "Well, I'd rather be running through canyons than driving with a gun in my back."

"Good. So how are we going to get up there?"

"I don't know. I thought this was *your* plan."

Scott finished pumping the gas and headed inside the station to pay. For a moment, he considered robbing the place. He rejected the idea. Another armed robbery would only tip off the police to his location. Once inside the dingy gas station, he glanced out the window toward the ladies' room door. There was no sign of the twins. He remembered the look of resolve he'd seen in Jessica's eyes, and he wondered if she was planning some sort of escape. Stupid girl. She couldn't get away from him.

A middle-aged man was staring at him curiously. "We don't get many strangers here, this time of year," the man said. "Off the beaten path and all that."

Scott grinned. "Yes, sir, it most certainly is." As he spoke, his eyes swept the place out of habit. One register. One employee. Not much business on New Year's Eve; the register was probably pretty empty, anyway. A black-and-white television set blared some silly game show from the corner of the room.

"My sisters and I are camping over by Lake Mead. They wanted to see some of this canyon country we'd heard about," he explained in a pleasant voice. "I wanted to stick to the main road, but that little sister of mine, she just loves to explore. You know how it is with women—it's easier to give in than to listen to them argue."

"Oh, don't I know it—" the man started to say. Then he put up a hand and turned to the television set. "Wait a minute. It's a special report on them service-station holdups around the state."

Scott froze. Under his jacket, his hand gripped a compact pistol—a Saturday night special he'd picked up at a pawnshop somewhere. Using the Colt would establish too strong a link between this and the last incident.

Damn! Scott thought. He'd hoped to lay low for a few days. But if the television station showed the surveillance film with Scott's picture, this man was as good as dead.

"A young woman is in critical condition at University Medical Center in Las Vegas after an early-morning shooting at a convenience store near the Moapa Indian reservation," said the grim-faced television announcer. "The FBI and local police departments are attempting to identify a suspect whose face appeared briefly on a surveillance video before the camera was shattered by gunshot."

Scott's finger moved to the trigger as the screen cut to the surveillance video.

First he saw the interior of the store, with the young, dark-haired clerk at the counter. Then the door opened and a figure walked in, wearing a light-colored Stetson. Scott almost laughed out loud. The person on the videotape was Jessica, her eyes widening with surprise and fear under the broad brim of the hat. The screen went blank.

"Officials are looking for a Caucasian female in her late teens," the announcer continued. "The suspect is of medium height, with a slender build and long, blond hair. She was last seen wearing a college T-shirt and blue jeans. Anyone who has information on her identity or whereabouts should contact the FBI's Carson City office, at the toll-free number on your screen."

Scott couldn't believe his luck. Jessica was the suspect. The only suspect.

"The suspect is also wanted for questioning in regard to a string of similar armed robberies throughout Nevada and Utah," the announcer continued. "She is armed and considered dangerous."

The gas-station attendant handed Scott his change. "Well, I'll be!" he said with a whistle. "Can you imagine a pretty little thing like that shooting up stores and killing people? You just never can tell who you can trust!"

"That's the truth," Scott said, pushing open the door and heading out into the bright sunlight. He certainly didn't trust Jessica and Elizabeth to follow his instructions. In fact, they still hadn't come out of the rest room. Scott knew exactly what they were up to.

Still grinning, he headed toward the ladies' room.

"Hurry, Elizabeth!" Jessica whispered frantically from the ground below the small window.

Elizabeth looked down at her from the window and began to squeeze her limbs through it. "I'm going as fast as I can!" she whispered back. "Remember, I didn't have anyone to give me a boost."

"Do you think he's still inside?" Jessica asked. "If he is, we might be able to make a run for the Jeep. Maybe he left the keys inside—"

"And maybe he didn't," Elizabeth said. "Here, catch me."

"Yeah, Jess," said Scott's calm voice. "Catch your sister. We wouldn't want her to get hurt now, would we?"

Elizabeth dropped to the ground, stunned. Scott was standing there, pointing a gun right at her. Wordlessly, Jessica reached out a hand to help her up, her eyes locked on the young, gray-eyed man. Elizabeth brushed the dirt off her jeans, staring curiously at Scott. Something was different. He seemed relaxed—happy, even.

"Ladies, ladies, ladies," he said, shaking his head in amused disapproval. "Didn't your parents ever teach you that it's not polite to leave without saying good-bye?"

He motioned with the gun, and Elizabeth fell

in step behind Jessica to trudge back to the Jeep. She sighed miserably. Their only hope for escape dwindled to the size of the tiny bird circling overhead in the harsh blue sky.

Jessica stared out the window at the passing scenery. Scott had ordered Elizabeth off the road and they were bumping along an unpaved trail, a cloud of reddish dust rising up around the Jeep. Crimson rock formed lumpy formations, jagged walls, towering natural chimneys, and soaring arches on both sides of the road. The taller ones were layered in burgundy, gray, mauve, and orange, along with the ever-present red that burned like flames.

"There's an area near here called the Valley of Fire," Scott explained in a conversational tone. "I remember a story—oh, about a hundred years ago—a fugitive Indian named Mouse used the place for his hideout."

Jessica stared at him. "How can you do this?"

"How can I do what?"

"Last night, you were kissing me. Now you're shooting people and holding a gun on us. But you still talk like we're the best of friends."

Scott grinned. "Never burn your bridges."

"Consider this one burned," Elizabeth told him in a cold voice.

Jessica winced. Provoking the man who was holding a gun on them didn't seem like the best course of action. Then she sighed and pressed her face against the window again.

What does it matter? He's going to kill us within the next few hours anyway. Do we really care whether it's here in the Jeep or underneath one of those creepy fire-rock things?

The fugitive-Indian part wasn't hard to believe. A fugitive like Scott could hide in a place like this for weeks, she thought. The eerie red rocks were probably riddled with so many caves and fissures that it would take the FBI months to search them all for a criminal—*or for two bodies.*

Jessica wiped a tear off her cheek, but more were spilling from her eyes faster than she could brush them away. In the seat in front of her, she could see Elizabeth's shoulders trembling with quiet sobs. Jessica hated to give up hope. But she knew that she and Elizabeth would never make it to Vail. And they would never again see their parents or their brother—or Tom, or Prince Albert, or even the dorm room in Dickenson Hall. Their parents would never even know what had happened to them.

Suddenly Jessica saw what looked like smoke in the distance. And it seemed to be coming closer. For a moment, she didn't understand what was happening. Then she heard the sound of an approaching train. Her body froze, but her mind raced in circles. Maybe Scott wasn't going to shoot them. Maybe he planned to kill them by pushing them in front of a train.

"Stop the Jeep here," Scott ordered. Jessica jumped out and ran to embrace her sister. Tears streamed down both their faces as Scott approached, his duffel bag over his shoulder and the gun gleaming silver in his hand. With the other hand, he grabbed Jessica's arm and wrenched her away from Elizabeth.

"One last time," he said as he pulled her toward him and kissed her roughly. For a moment, Jessica found herself responding to his moist, insistent lips. Then she yanked herself away from him, wiping her mouth on her arm.

Scott laughed. The train was approaching—a big, noisy freight train.

Jessica felt dizzy. In another minute, she and Elizabeth would be dead. She looked into Scott's gray eyes and saw a hunger in them that frightened her.

Then the train was roaring by them. Scott turned away from them, almost reluctantly. He ran a few paces toward the speeding train and jumped into the air, grabbing hold of a railing on the side of a partly opened car.

Then he was gone, in a cloud of red dust and gray smoke. Jessica collapsed into Elizabeth's arms, crying with relief as the train disappeared between craggy red cliffs.

Scott laughed out loud as he peered back through the dust that spiraled into the air around the freight train. Jessica and Elizabeth had looked about as relieved as two people could be, he thought with some satisfaction. He coughed and fanned the dust away from his face.

Elation filled him—the same kind of elation that overwhelmed him every time he saw fear in the eyes of someone he was about to blow away. It didn't matter whether he decided to let people live or to kill them. The elation was in the power to choose life or death for others. It was a power that could cause terror in other people. There was nothing in the world like that rush of sheer power.

"Damn!" he said suddenly, still choking on dust. "I forgot my lucky Stetson." Oh, well, there was no going back for it now. "Let Jessica keep it," he said aloud. "It'll be a little something to remember me by."

Through the dust, he watched the twins flying back to the Jeep as if their feet had wings. He coughed again and dove into the dimness of the empty freight car. He knotted the faded blue bandanna around his neck and pulled it up to cover his nose. Then he rested against a bale of hay and imagined the twins' next move.

"They'll jump in that little black Jeep of theirs," he said to the empty freight car, "and they'll rush off to the nearest town to report me to the authorities. And as soon as they step into the police station, they'll be nailed!"

Scott smiled as he poked the gun back into his

canvas duffel bag. The police would arrest the twins for the robbery of the Moapa store. The FBI probably couldn't pin the other crimes on the twins. But an attempted-murder charge would be enough to keep Jessica and Elizabeth busy answering questions for a long, long time.

"Oh, the cops might figure out what really happened, eventually," Scott decided. "But by then, I'll be in Mexico."

And if Jessica and Elizabeth had to spend some time in jail in the meantime, that was their problem.

Chapter Seven

Jeff grabbed the telephone on the first ring.

"I'm in Sweet Valley," came Keisha's voice. "But so far, I've had no luck finding our suspect's name—"

"Elizabeth Wakefield," Jeff supplied. "And I've been doing some digging on her. She's eighteen and a freshman there. And she doesn't fit the profile for armed robbery at all."

"Does she have a police record?"

"None at all. In fact, she's got excellent grades and is a student journalist. She comes from a supportive family and an upper-middle-class background. Both parents are professionals."

He could practically hear Keisha's pretty face fall into a frown. "That does sound odd. Are you sure she's our suspect?"

"Well, not completely. Her picture was in the local newspaper a couple years ago; it sure looks like the girl on the surveillance video."

"Is there any tie-in with the Jeep that was spotted?"

"I found a record of a black Jeep registered to her and a sister—Jessica. That's the problem. She and her sister are twins."

"If they're identical, then it could just as easily be Jessica we're looking for."

"Right. But it has to be one or the other. The girl in the newspaper clipping looks exactly like the one on our videotape."

"What do you know about the sister? Does she sound any more likely as an armed-robbery suspect?"

"Not really," Jeff said. "Jessica's not an honor student like Elizabeth. But she's never been in any serious trouble. She was a high school cheerleader—a sorority type."

"Do you want me to run a check on them through FBI records?"

"I already did," Jeff said. "That's another funny thing. Both girls actually *helped* the Bureau bring in a drug dealer a few years back."

"They don't sound like violent criminals," Keisha remarked.

Jeff shrugged. "No, they don't. But I'm positive that it's one of them on the video."

"As you said before, tapes don't lie," Keisha said. "Have you located their parents?"

"I sent someone to the house, but the parents

seem to be on vacation. We've got an agent looking for them, but I want you to work another angle. Find the twins' dorm room on campus and pay them a little visit. Maybe one of them is there."

"No such luck, Jeff," Keisha said. "The dorms are closed up tight for winter break. Even the students aren't allowed in."

Jeff sighed. "Okay, then try this one. The twins have a brother who's a prelaw student at SVU. His name's Steven—find him. Maybe he knows what his sister is up to."

"Do you want me to follow up on the Jeep as well?"

"I already sent the license number on to the interstate patrols. But I don't think we're going to find that Jeep at a roadblock—she's too smart for that. I think she's heading cross-country."

"So what's your next step?"

"I wanted to run over to the hospital in Vegas."

"Has the clerk from the Moapa store regained consciousness?"

"I don't know. But if she's able to talk, I want to question her. Call me if you learn anything new."

After Jeff hung up, he stared at the videotaped picture of the Wakefield girl, as if it might hold some clue he had missed so far. Without meaning to, he found himself gazing into her large, clear eyes. No matter how hard he tried, he couldn't look into those eyes and feel hatred. And it wasn't only the fact that Elizabeth—or Jessica—Wakefield was beautiful, with Summer's eyes. The more he learned about the twins, the more confused he felt. The pain he'd felt since Summer's death only intensified when he looked at the photograph of his suspect.

Jeff took a deep breath. His personal feelings were irrelevant. He had a job to do, and he would do it. It was as simple as that.

Elizabeth watched the horizon for signs of a town as Jessica drove wildly over the bumpy gravel road. With every jolt, the too-big Stetson jiggled from side to side on Jessica's head. The road seemed to be climbing to a rugged area of high plateaus and half-shadowed mountains.

"Can't you figure it out on the map?" Jessica asked, straightening the hat. "You're supposed to be good with maps."

Elizabeth sighed. "Maps are useless if you don't know where you are to begin with. I'm not even sure what state we're in. The sun's beginning to set directly behind us, so that means we're heading east. We might have crossed the Arizona border by now. Or we may still be in Nevada."

Jessica wrinkled her nose. "Arizona? I thought Arizona was a desert! These are practically mountains!"

Elizabeth shook her head. Usually she was amused by Jessica's confusion about geography. But now that the twins were over their initial, giddy relief at being alive and free of Scott, she was beginning to worry. And Jessica seemed almost hysterical.

"The area north of the Grand Canyon is actually pretty mountainous," she said, hoping her voice was steady. "In fact, I remember reading that the elevation is about as high as Denver."

"You're making fun of me. It could never be this cold in Arizona."

"It gets cold in northern Arizona at this time of year. There's usually snow. But maybe we won't run into any because of the heat wave." She shivered. "You're right about it being cold. We could stop and get our warmer clothes out of the suitcase."

"Not now," Jessica said grimly. "We have to get to a town." Elizabeth saw that she was pushing against the steering wheel as if that would help them arrive faster. "There was a surveillance camera in that store. The police will be looking for Scott for attempted murder. We have to tell them where he is before he can hurt anyone else!"

"How can we tell anyone where Scott is?" Elizabeth asked hopelessly. "We don't even know where *we* are."

"You're supposed to be the smart one!" Jessica yelled. "Figure it out!"

Elizabeth stared at her, shocked.

Jessica sighed. "I'm sorry, Liz. It's not your fault. It's my fault. I insisted on giving him a ride. And I watched him shoot that woman. . . ." She bit her lip.

"It's all right, Jess," Elizabeth said. She was inclined to agree that her twin was mostly responsible for their predicament. But Jessica seemed volatile right now. Agreeing that she was to blame for all their problems might make her panic. *At least I can accomplish something by comforting Jessica,* she thought. Elizabeth hated feeling helpless.

"I'm as much to blame as you are," she said. "I shouldn't have let you talk me into giving him a ride. But we had no way of knowing what he was really like. I'm just grateful we're both alive and all right."

Jessica nodded and looked a little happier.

"And you can't blame yourself for that woman in the store—" Elizabeth broke off, looking around with growing excitement.

"Liz, what is it?"

"Am I imagining things, or is this road getting better? Look up ahead—it's a paved road! I bet it leads to a town!"

Jessica bounced in the seat, staring through the windshield. The hat jumped on her head. "Yes, there it is! There's a town. Oh, Liz, thank God. I was so scared we'd run out of gas in the middle of nowhere, and then we'd die of thirst in those creepy fire canyons, and nobody would ever find us."

Elizabeth sank back into her seat, relieved. In just a few more minutes, they would find the local police station and tell the authorities all about Scott. Their ordeal would be over.

Jeff drove east along the interstate from Las Vegas, heading back toward Moapa. His car phone rang—or rather, it emitted an annoying electronic chirping noise. Sometimes the FBI's high-tech gadgetry was just plain irritating, even when it allowed him a range that was much farther than that of a regular cellular phone.

"Jeff, it's Keisha, still in California," came the agent's voice, crackling with static because of the long-distance connection. "I just had a long talk with Steven Wakefield. He and his sisters were supposed to go skiing together this week, at Vail. But the poor guy got the flu and had to stay home."

"Does that mean the girls are together? Are they on their way to Colorado?"

"That was the plan," Keisha said. "They're expected to arrive tonight. And he's positively identified the photograph from the surveillance video. It's not Elizabeth. It's Jessica."

"How the heck does he know? They're identical."

"He's their brother. He can tell his own sisters apart."

Jeff shrugged. "I guess so. What else did he tell you?"

"That I was insane. He says Jessica has a bit of a wild streak—but dating two guys on the same night is a far cry from armed robbery and attempted murder."

"First-degree murder," Jeff corrected her bitterly.

"Jeff," Keisha said, "I know how badly you want to find the person who killed Summer. But we have no evidence to link this morning's shooting to the one in Stillwater—or to any of the others, for that matter. It's possible that Jessica Wakefield just hit this one store. She might not be Summer's killer."

"I'm absolutely positive that all these holdups are connected."

"I'm sorry, Jeff, but Steven Wakefield says Jessica was in California at the time of Summer's death. So a first-degree-murder charge is out of the question right now."

"Maybe she can't be charged with Summer's murder yet," he said, "but I just left University Medical Center in Las Vegas. The clerk from the holdup this morning died."

Silence passed over the phone line between them. Finally Keisha took a deep breath and said, "I know you were counting on her to tell you what really happened in that store today. I'm sorry you've lost another witness."

"I'm sorry about losing anybody to senseless violence," Jeff said quietly. "So when we find Jessica Wakefield, the charge is first-degree murder."

Jeff hung up the phone and glanced again at Jessica's picture on the seat next to him. He pounded the steering wheel. "Does she have to be so gorgeous?" he muttered under his breath. Steven Wakefield was right. He *was* insane—not to mention unprofessional. "I'm supposed to hate the criminal I'm tracking," he whispered. "Not fall in love with her."

But his instincts told him there was more going on here than the surveillance video showed. Jessica Wakefield was innocent. He was sure of it.

The phone chirped. "What else, Keish?" he asked impatiently.

"It's not Keisha," came the voice of one of his assistants. "I've just spoken with the state police."

"Have the roadblocks picked up anything?"

"Nada. But there's a report of a black Jeep that fits the description, crossing into Arizona on a gravel road in the area north of Lake Mead."

"When?"

"A few hours ago," the agent said ruefully. "Sorry I can't be more exact. It was a local cop who saw the Jeep. He didn't think much of it until he heard the all-points bulletin."

"Did he catch the license plate number? Did he see who was inside?"

"None of the above. He only noticed the Jeep at all because it's unusual for someone to be driving along those trails this time of year."

"See if you can get me the exact time and location of the sighting," Jeff said.

He could hear the hesitation in his assistant's voice. "There's one other thing."

"What is it?"

"The California highway patrol found an abandoned car broken down by the side of Interstate 15, with a busted radiator. It was between Baker and the Nevada border."

"So?"

"It's a beat-up Oldsmobile sedan. It's light blue—or it was once—and it's fifteen years old. We can't be sure, but it does fit the description of the one you've been after. I thought you'd want to know."

Jeff's eyes narrowed. In his excitement about having identified one vehicle, he had completely forgotten about the old sedan.

"If this Olds really is linked with some of the other robberies," the assistant continued, "then I guess we can rule out any connection between those robberies and the one this morning. We've already tied the black Jeep to that one."

"That doesn't mean anything. Our perpetrator could have switched cars, just to throw us off the track."

"Jeff, the Olds was facing west, heading into California. The Wakefields are clearly heading east. They can't be going in two directions at once. The only explanation is that the Moapa store wasn't robbed by the same person as the others."

"Yes, it was," Jeff insisted. "I intend to prove that all of these cases are linked."

"But with this new evidence, it just doesn't make sense."

"It doesn't make sense?" Jeff snapped. "It makes as much sense as two squeaky-clean college students taking time out from a ski vacation to go on an armed-robbery spree!"

Jeff suddenly realized he was yelling at the agent. "Sorry. I didn't mean to go ballistic. Were there any clues on the Oldsmobile?"

"There isn't a single fingerprint anywhere. The highway patrol thinks it was wiped clean."

"What about the license plate?"

"It's no help at all. It was ripped off of a car in Nevada last week. But I'm running a check on the vehicle ID number through Washington. I'll let you know if it turns up anything."

"Okay," Jeff said. "For now, I guess our best bet is still to follow the Jeep. Until further notice, pull your patrols off the California border. Mobilize everyone you can find in northwest Arizona and southwest Utah."

"Any idea where they're going?"

"Keisha says the twins' original destination was

Vail. I doubt they'll still try to make it there, but that Jeep is obviously heading east."

"Are you on your way there, too?"

"I have to stop by the field office first, but then I'll head to the border." Jeff swerved to avoid a car whose turn signal he should have noticed sooner. This case had him so preoccupied that he could hardly think straight, let alone drive straight.

"And remind your people that these girls are innocent until proven guilty," he said in a soft voice. "I want to bring them in unharmed."

"Of course," the agent said. "But, Jeff, there is something you should know. . . ."

The note of concern in his voice made Jeff sit up straighter. "What?"

"I can keep a tight rein on our own agents. But it's all over the news that the clerk from Moapa died an hour ago. Some of these local cops are pretty hot under the collar about this case."

"What do you mean?"

"They're talking like they're an Old West posse. I can make your instructions clear, Jeff. But I can't guarantee that someone's trigger finger won't get itchy at the wrong moment."

Jeff hung up the phone, his thoughts racing. He'd tried to keep the clerk's death from the press. Knowing that the charge was first-degree murder could make the twins desperate. And inexperienced criminals tended to kill people when they got desperate, or to get themselves killed.

But he'd failed to keep the news under wraps. The hospital had been full of reporters, and this was exactly the kind of case that made headlines. Jeff could picture it now: TWIN COEDS WANTED FOR MURDER.

A sick feeling rose from the pit of his stomach. His assistant had been right—cases that made headlines also made careers for small-town law-enforcement officials. Every cop in northwest Arizona would be out there, hoping to be the one who brought in the stunning, armed-and-dangerous Wakefield twins. Dead or alive.

"I have to get there first," Jeff said aloud, not able to clear his mind of the image of beautiful Jessica Wakefield in the Stetson hat. "It's the only way we'll ever learn the truth."

He pressed the gas pedal and willed the Mustang to fly. It was already five thirty in the evening. He had to get to Arizona fast. He had to be the one who located Jessica and Elizabeth Wakefield. If the local police found the twins before he did, they would shoot first and ask questions later.

Tom slammed the phone back onto its hook. Then he sank into a chair in the hotel room he was sharing with Danny.

Danny's voice came from behind a skiing magazine. "I take it the front desk told you Elizabeth hasn't checked in since you called ten minutes ago."

"Where is she?" Tom demanded.

Danny lowered the magazine to give his room-mate the full benefit of the exasperated expression on his face. "What do you mean, where is she? If I know Elizabeth, she's exactly where she's supposed to be. She's somewhere between Grand Junction and here, driving as fast as possible so she'll meet us in time for the party."

"If everything's okay, then why didn't she call back?"

"Why should she? You know they didn't get as far as they'd expected last night. So it's going to take them a little longer to get here tonight. Relax."

"How can I relax when Elizabeth is late? She may be in danger!"

"She is not late, Tom. We weren't expecting the twins until eight o'clock anyway. It's only six thirty." Danny laughed. "Take a lesson from me, Tom. Isabella said she'd meet us in our room a half hour ago. She's not here yet. But do I look worried?"

Tom rolled his eyes. "Give me a break. Isabella's not out in the middle of a desert some-where; she's in her own room across the hall. Besides, Isabella's never been ready on time in her entire life. You know how punctual Elizabeth is."

"That's right. And she said she'd be here be-tween eight and eight thirty. So why don't you

144

wait until then to become a basket case?"

"Danny, if you had heard that phone conversation this morning . . . I'm sure I heard gunshots in the background."

"Are you really sure?"

Tom stared at him for a moment. "No," he admitted. "I'm not positive. It may have been a car backfiring. There was a lot of static on the line, and I couldn't really hear anything well."

"Then why are you jumping to the worst possible conclusions?"

"Because I heard about another roadside robbery just before we left California. It happened right around the time Elizabeth called, in southern Nevada somewhere."

"Yeah, I heard about that one too. A woman was shot—I heard she wasn't expected to live. But the report gave her name, and it wasn't Wakefield."

Tom sighed. "I know. I'm being unreasonable. But I can't help it—I just have this tight feeling in my chest, like I'm going to choke."

"Maybe you caught Steven's flu."

"No, it's not that. It reminds me of that twins' ESP Elizabeth and Jessica claim to have— you know, each one can tell when the other's in trouble."

"Elizabeth's not in trouble, Tom, and you're not her twin. You're her boyfriend—her *ex*-boyfriend, if you keep treating her like a twelve-year-old. Look, she'll be here soon. Just don't think about it."

"You're right. I guess I'll turn on the TV," Tom decided. "I hope they've got an all-news station around here."

Jessica drove slowly down the main street of the town. "I don't see a police station anywhere!" she cried as she reached the last block and turned around for the second time. "Maybe it's on one of the side streets."

"I didn't see one either," Elizabeth said.

"I think we should keep driving. That sign says Diamond Butte is a few miles farther—maybe that has a police station."

"We don't even know if that's the name of a town! We have no idea where we are—it seems stupid to just keep driving in circles. Let's look around here a little more. Maybe we can ask someone where the nearest police station is."

Jessica shrugged. "Okay. One podunk town seems as good as any other to me. Let's go back to the restaurant we passed a few seconds ago." She wheeled into a parking space and slammed on the breaks. The Jeep skidded to a stop.

"Maybe you should let me drive next time," Elizabeth suggested.

"Come on—let's go find somebody to report Scott to. That restaurant was only a block back, right?"

"Right," said Elizabeth. "And it's about dinnertime. There ought to be plenty of people there to get directions from."

"Speaking of dinner," Jessica said, "we should grab something to eat as long as we're near a restaurant. I'm starving."

"Me too," Elizabeth agreed. "But I want to talk to the police first."

Jessica threw the Stetson on the seat as she clambered out of the Jeep. Then the twins hurried back along the street, squinting into the technicolor light of the setting sun.

"It's getting chilly," Elizabeth said. "Let's pull out some of our Colorado clothes as soon as we talk to the police. Where's the restaurant?"

"It's up there," Jessica said. "Right after this television store." She glanced at a TV screen in the window and stopped so abruptly that Elizabeth walked into her.

"What's wrong?" Elizabeth asked. "Why are we stopping?"

Jessica pointed to the TV. A red-haired reporter was standing in a parking lot, speaking into a microphone. "Elizabeth, look at the building behind the reporter. That's the store Scott held up this morning!"

"You're right," Elizabeth said. "Let's go in and see what they're saying about him."

Jessica pushed open the door. She jumped when something jingled close by. *I must really be on edge,* she thought. *Even bells are scaring me now.*

"I'll be right with you," called a man's voice from a room behind the counter. "Feel free to browse."

The twins stood in front of a row of television sets, all tuned to the evening news.

"The victim died this afternoon at University Medical Center in Las Vegas," the reporter said. "In response to her death, the authorities have raised the charge to first-degree murder. Police say the store's surveillance camera was shot out just before the robbery—but not until after the camera had caught the suspect on film. Now we'll cut to actual footage from that surveillance video."

First the screen showed footage of the interior of the store. Jessica nodded. Yes, that was exactly what it had looked like. Then a figure in a Stetson hat walked in. A gun gleamed. The twins watched, breathless, as the camera caught the suspect's face under the hat brim. Jessica's face, with frightened eyes and long, golden hair. The tape ended abruptly.

Jessica began to tremble. "Oh, God, Liz. Oh, God."

Elizabeth took a deep breath, but her voice still came out in a whisper. "Scott must've been hidden by that stupid hat. The camera didn't pick him up at all."

Jessica felt rooted to the linoleum floor. "Oh, my God, Liz. That means they're not looking for Scott at all. They're looking for me."

Elizabeth glanced back behind the counter. "You mean they're looking for us," she corrected in a whisper. "Remember, we're identical. Let's get out of here before anyone sees us." She half-dragged Jessica to the door, and they began walking the one block back to the Jeep.

Jessica stopped suddenly and grabbed Elizabeth's arm. A black-and-white car was parked on a nearby side street. "Elizabeth!" she hissed. "The police are here!" She looked around frantically.

"Oh, God, Liz. Don't turn around! There are two police officers following us. And another one heading this way from across the street. What do we do?"

Elizabeth took a deep breath. "Turn ourselves in, I guess. If we just explain—"

"Turn ourselves in?" Jessica screeched, walking faster. "Are you deranged?"

A whistle trilled behind them. "This is the police!" shouted a man's voice. "Put your hands up. If you reach for your weapons, we will shoot."

Later, Jessica remembered the next five minutes as if they had passed in slow motion. She turned her head just enough to see that there was no sign of sympathy in the officers' faces. Each one had a gun trained on Jessica and Elizabeth. At the sight of the guns, Jessica sprang into action.

"Into the Jeep!" she whispered wildly, pushing

her sister in front of her. She grabbed the door handle and shoved Elizabeth in. Then she raced to the driver's door and dove in herself as one of the police officers opened fire. Jessica squeezed the Jeep out of the parking space and careened down the street, away from the brilliant sunset. In the rearview mirror, she saw the officers running to their patrol car.

"Stop, Jessica," Elizabeth stammered. "Oh, my God. I can't believe we're running from the police."

"They'll never believe us!" Jessica wailed. "I'm on the videotape, not Scott. Don't you see, Liz? Don't you get it? We're wanted for murder, Elizabeth! We've got to escape!"

From somewhere behind them, Jessica heard the whine of a siren.

"Okay," Elizabeth said, visibly trying to pull herself together. "You're right. But how will we get away from them? This is the only road. They'll radio ahead to another police car and—"

The Jeep was passing a tall slab of sandstone that glowed like blood in the sunset. As she whipped past it, Jessica turned the steering wheel hard.

"Jessica!" Elizabeth screamed.

For a moment, Jessica thought she'd miscalculated. The face of the sandstone cliff raced toward the windshield. Then it passed to her right, just inches away. The Jeep was speeding away from the main road on a narrow path that ran between rocky cliffs and buttes.

"Where are they?" she asked breathlessly. "Are they following us?"

Elizabeth knelt on the seat, watching through the back window. "No," she said finally, taking a deep breath. "They just rushed right past this path. But keep going! They may not have given up yet."

Jessica nodded and steered the Jeep off the road into a snaky canyon between two high walls of rock. "This place is like a maze," she said after she'd been driving a while longer. "They'll never find us here. Let's stop for a few minutes now and figure out a plan."

"Jessica, we can't hide forever."

"Easy for you to say! It's not your face on TV. Elizabeth, that video makes it look like *I* robbed the store—and murdered the clerk!"

Elizabeth shrugged. "It might as well be my face. If it looks like it was you, then it looks like it was me. We're definitely in this together."

"So why do you want to give ourselves up?"

"That's not what I meant. If they find us, we're doomed!"

Jessica scowled at her. "So you don't want to hide, and you don't want to be found. Real helpful, Liz."

"We've got to find Scott."

Jessica stared at her sister in astonishment.

Elizabeth had finally lost it. "Did you hit your head on the ceiling, going over some of those bumps?"

"I'm trying to be reasonable," Elizabeth said, "unlike you. You're beginning to sound hysterical."

"Scott's the one who got us into this mess in the first place!"

"That's why we need to find him—so he can get us out of it."

"Get a clue, Liz! If you were 'being reasonable,' you'd be terrified of Scott. He could have killed us!"

"But he didn't."

"Liz, you didn't see his eyes when he kissed me, before he jumped on that train." She shivered with more than the cold. "In that moment, I thought I finally understood him. I don't know if I can explain it, but I saw this awful hunger in his eyes, like he could never be satisfied."

"Satisfied?"

"Well, yes. It was like he could never get enough, as if he loved having so much power over us, and as if he liked the danger."

Elizabeth looked at her strangely. "I know he's dangerous, Jess. But I don't think we have any choice. We—"

"Aren't we in enough trouble already?" Jessica interrupted tearfully. "Do you have to go out to look for more?"

Elizabeth rested a hand on Jessica's shoulder. "Jessica, listen to me. There's only one person alive who knows we didn't shoot that woman in the store. And like it or not, that person is Scott!"

"Great. So all we have to do is find one armed murderer who doesn't want to be found, somewhere in the middle of this wasteland. Even if we can find him, then what do we do? Do you really expect him to turn himself in if we ask nicely?"

"Of course he's not going to turn himself in. We'll have to trick him, or lead the police to him somehow."

"Right," Jessica said sarcastically. "Piece of cake."

"Come on, Jessica! You're the one who's good at thinking up schemes. You got us away from the police. Now help me find Scott and get him *to* the police."

Elizabeth was staring at her with a pleading look in her blue-green eyes. Jessica sighed.

She started the Jeep, trying to keep her hands from trembling. As usual, Elizabeth was right. There was only one way out of this.

They had to find Scott and bring him to justice.

Chapter
Eight

Tom was slumped across one of the beds in his hotel room at Vail. He had been staring at the TV for a half hour without really seeing it. In the corner of the room, Danny and Isabella were studying a map of the slopes.

Suddenly a snatch of conversation on the news made him sit up straight. His friends looked up from their map. "What is it?" Isabella asked, pushing a lock of tousled black hair away from her face.

"Shhh!" Tom hissed as the news cut to an exterior shot of a roadside convenience store. "This is the place that was held up this morning."

"A young woman is dead at a Las Vegas hospital tonight, after being shot in an armed robbery at this store along Interstate 15," the man said. "The woman was the only employee working when the holdup occurred. Local police are working with the FBI to locate a suspect whose picture was captured by a video surveillance camera just before the camera was shot out. Now, let's cut to that dramatic video footage."

Tom held his breath as the camera panned the inside of the clean, modern store. A young woman with long dark hair stood behind the counter, making a pot of coffee. Then the door swung open and somebody walked in, silhouetted black against the early-morning sunlight. The light reflected off the barrel of a revolver. Tom could see that the suspect was wearing a Stetson hat, but it was a moment longer before the person's face was visible beneath it.

"Jessica!" gasped Tom, Danny, and Isabella in unison.

"The FBI has identified the young woman in the video as eighteen-year-old Jessica Wakefield of Sweet Valley, California," announced the reporter. "She is thought to be traveling east with her twin sister, Elizabeth. The women are being sought for first-degree-murder charges, as well as for questioning in several similar holdups across Nevada and Utah. They are armed and considered extremely dangerous. Anyone with information on the whereabouts of the Wakefield twins should contact the FBI office in Carson City, at the number that appears on your screen."

"That's ridiculous!" blurted Isabella as the program moved on to a story about a fire in Denver. "Jessica's no criminal!"

Tom felt numb all over. This was it—the reason for the wave of dread that had been threatening to overcome him for the last two days. Forcing his hand to move, he reached for the telephone, the FBI number emblazoned across his mind.

Jeff strapped on his shoulder holster and prepared to leave the Moapa field office. He was stopped by the ringing of the telephone. He glanced around for the temporary secretary or another of the agents who he knew were somewhere in the building. But the room was empty. Reluctantly, Jeff picked up the phone.

"Jeff, I've got a call here from somebody who saw the video and a report about the Wakefields on television," said his secretary in Carson City.

"I'm on my way out the door. I don't need to talk with every crackpot who—"

"This 'crackpot' is calling from a resort in Vail, Colorado. He says that his name is Tom Watts—and that he's Elizabeth Wakefield's boyfriend."

Jeff sat down quickly. "Are you verifying his name and location?"

"I'm running a trace on the call."

"Good. Patch him through."

"What the heck is going on with you people?"

a young man's voice demanded. Apparently Elizabeth's boyfriend was not pleased with the FBI's investigation.

"Calm down, for pete's sake," Jeff said. "What do you know about this?"

"I know that Jessica Wakefield is about as likely to commit armed robbery as she is to ace an advanced calculus test! I don't know where the FBI gets its information, but I know the Wakefields. And they're not criminals!"

"I said to calm down!" Jeff repeated sternly. "Getting emotional isn't going to help. You saw the surveillance video. Tell me, was it or was it not Jessica Wakefield?"

Tom sighed. "It was Jessica, all right—though she didn't have that hat when she left California."

"You're sure it wasn't Elizabeth?"

"Of course I'm sure. I know my own girlfriend!"

"In what ways do they look different?"

"Jess always leaves her hair down, and she wears more makeup than Liz. And their facial expressions are all different."

"Anything else?"

"I told you it was Jessica! Besides, Elizabeth is even less capable of violence than her sister. There is no way either one of those twins robbed a store or shot someone!"

"You saw the tape," Jeff reminded him

again. "If the Wakefields didn't rob that store, then why did the camera catch Jessica with a gun?"

"Obviously the tape is wrong—or you missed something on it. How the heck should I know? Isn't that your job?"

"Look, son," Jeff said in the most soothing voice he could muster. He realized with a start that it was the first time he'd ever called a college student "son." This case was making him feel older by the minute. "If you want to help your girlfriend, you'll tell the FBI everything you know about the Wakefields and their trip."

"Why in the world would I want to do that?"

"So I can bring them in safely, before some of these local police departments train their sights on them. Will you help me find them?"

"The hell I will!"

"I have to warn you," Jeff continued calmly, "that if you refuse to help, you'll look like an accomplice in the death of that store clerk. We may have to bring you in for questioning."

"You do what you have to!" Tom cried. A loud click made Jeff jump. Tom had hung up on him.

"Did you get enough for a trace?" Jeff asked the secretary.

"I sure did. We should have the name of his hotel in Vail within a few seconds. Do you want me to send someone there?"

Jeff thought for a moment. "Keisha's pretty much finished in Sweet Valley. Book her on the next flight to Vail."

"Do you want me to call the Denver office to get some agents in Colorado to back her up?"

"You read my mind. Have them set up a temporary office somewhere in the hotel. Also, I want everything you can find on Tom Watts."

Jeff put down the phone and once again picked up Jessica Wakefield's photograph. He didn't want to admit it, but Tom Watts had gotten to him. The young man's belief in the twins' innocence was sincere. And his doubts about the videotape echoed Jeff's own doubts. Jessica's frightened eyes were not the eyes of a killer. Now they stared at him accusingly.

Obviously the tape is wrong, Jessica seemed to be saying. *Or you missed something on it.*

Jeff recognized the words as Tom's. Well, maybe the surveillance video warranted another look.

"I'm glad we're on a real road again," said Elizabeth, at the wheel of the Jeep. "But do you hear a funny noise in the engine—kind of a knocking? I wonder if we tore something loose, crossing all that rough terrain?"

Jessica shook her head. "Don't even think it! We're in the middle of nowhere. It's dark and cold, and we haven't seen a house or a gas station in ages. Plus, we haven't eaten since breakfast, and we don't have any water."

"I know. I'm hungry too—" Elizabeth began, but Jessica kept talking.

"Besides that, the police are after us. And to top it all off, we're searching like crazy to find a dangerous criminal who might kill us—but we have no idea where to look. A broken-down car would pretty much put the cap on a perfect day, don't you think?"

Elizabeth shot a dark glance at her sister. *Jessica's a fine one to complain*, she thought. *If she hadn't insisted on giving Scott a lift in the first place* . . . She shoved the thought from her mind again.

"Do you have any idea where we are?" Jessica asked.

"Some," Elizabeth replied, feeling her spirits lift a little at the knowledge. "When it was still light enough to see some of the countryside, I was trying to compare what was around us to what's on the map. I think I can pinpoint our location to within a few dozen miles."

"And where would that be?" Jessica asked impatiently.

"I think we're in Arizona, north of the Grand Canyon. And we're running parallel to railroad tracks from that place where Scott jumped the train. Maybe he'll have stopped in the next town."

161

"We'll probably freeze before we get there," Jessica said glumly, hugging herself for warmth, despite the heavy sweater she had finally pulled out of her suitcase.

"We're lucky we haven't hit any snow yet," Elizabeth told her. "Don't be surprised if we run into some. This area usually has a good amount of it by this time of year."

"How can it be so hot in the morning and so cold at night?"

Elizabeth shrugged. "What do I look like, a meteorologist?"

"You don't have to be so nasty about it."

"I'm not being nasty," Elizabeth snapped. "I can't help it if this isn't my idea of a fun New Year's Eve."

Jessica's face fell, and Elizabeth was afraid she'd start to cry. "New Year's Eve," Jessica repeated in a stunned voice. "I completely forgot about it. What a way to spend New Year's Eve! I was going to dance all night with cute skiers—"

Elizabeth smiled ruefully. "And now you're stuck with just me."

"What time is it, anyway?"

Elizabeth flicked on the overhead light to check her watch. "Only seven thirty!" she exclaimed. "I could have sworn it was later. It sure gets dark out here, with no lights anywhere." Then she remembered something. "Oh, it's really eight thirty! Arizona's in a later time zone than Nevada."

162

Jessica rolled her eyes. "Who cares? It's a crummy way to spend New Year's Eve in any time zone."

For the fifth time in half an hour, Jeff watched Jessica Wakefield walk into the Moapa convenience store, wearing the Stetson hat. But for some reason, it was the hat that caught his eye this time, once he tore his gaze from her lovely, innocent-looking face.

"Fran!" he called to the woman at the other end of the temporary field office. "You're the resident video guru," he said as she came toward him. "Take a look at this one for me."

The video technician sat on the edge of his desk. "Do you really think you're going to see something different in it this time? Wishful thinking isn't going to help, Jeff."

Few technical specialists would talk to the lead agent in the state's main office that way, he reflected. But he and Fran had been friends since college. He had relied many times in the past on her expertise and her unique perspective. Now he needed her more than ever.

"Humor me," he said simply. Wishful thinking or not, he was sure he had spotted something different in the tape. But he needed confirmation. Jeff played back the surveillance tape again.

"Watch the crown of her hat in this next part,"

he ordered. "I could've sworn I saw some sort of shadow behind the hat."

"Replay that again at half speed," Fran said thoughtfully.

"What do you think that shadow is?" Jeff asked.

Fran pursed her lips. "I'm not sure. Play it again. I want to stop the darn thing at exactly the right point."

"That's it!" Jeff cried when she paused the video. He jumped from his seat to gesture toward one part of the image. "There's a second person back there!" For the first time in weeks, Jeff felt some hope. "I'm sure there's a man behind her! Maybe he's the one whose hand is on the gun. Maybe he was pushing Jessica in front of him."

"It's possible," Fran admitted. "It's hard to see him, as dim as it is in that part of the store."

"And with that hat she's wearing, you'd be hard-pressed to pick him out on the tape if you weren't watching for him."

"I think you're right," Fran said. "But I can't be absolutely certain. The image is much too dark. Let me blow it up and use the lab to enhance that part of it. Then I'll be able to tell you more."

Jeff scowled and checked his watch. It was late, and he wanted to get on the road to get closer to the Wakefields' location. Unfortunately, he still didn't know just where that was.

"Relax, Mr. Special Agent on a Mission," Fran told him. She spoke lightly, but her eyes were full of concern. Obviously he wasn't doing a very good job of maintaining a professional demeanor. "This will take only a few minutes."

Jeff nodded and tried to follow her advice. But with every tick of his watch, Jessica and Elizabeth Wakefield were moving farther away from him. He tried to imagine what they were thinking as he watched the door of the dark room where Fran worked on enlarging the image.

Jeff had never met Jessica, but he was beginning to feel very close to her. Jessica was impulsive and inclined to action, Jeff had learned from the transcript of Keisha's interview with Steven Wakefield. Summer had been just as irrepressible. Elizabeth was more practical, he reminded himself. She would think first and weigh all the options before acting. Elizabeth was his best hope for keeping her sister in check, until Jeff himself could reach them.

But if the police got to the girls first, Jessica might act without thinking. She might run. The police thought she was an armed and dangerous criminal. If she fled, they would shoot. Jeff closed his eyes against a mental image of Summer's bullet-riddled body at the morgue— but in his mind, the figure now had Jessica's golden hair.

"What is it, Jeff?" Fran asked, shaking him gently. "I've been calling you for five minutes. You look like you've seen a ghost."

Jeff blinked. "Sorry. I guess I was kind of preoccupied."

"To tell you the truth, Jeff, I'm worried about you. I've never seen you in so much pain. You haven't had a single moment of peace in two weeks."

Jeff shrugged off her concern. *Peace?* he asked himself. *That's a laugh.* He was sure he would never be at peace again.

But his personal pain didn't matter. The only thing that mattered was finding the person or persons who killed Summer and the store clerk. "Did you get the enhancement finished?" he asked brusquely.

"That's what I was trying to tell you," she replied quietly. "Here, take a look. There *is* a man behind the sweet young thing in the hat."

"The picture's kind of fuzzy, but it might be clear enough for someone to identify him," Jeff said.

"Do you want me to get his picture and description out over the wire?"

Jeff nodded, staring into the steely eyes of the man he was sure had killed the young Paiute clerk. Suddenly he knew in the pit of his stomach that the same man had killed Summer O'Brian.

"So what's the enigmatic expression on your face?" Fran asked. Jeff was grateful for her light tone. "I don't suppose you're thinking, 'Fran is the most marvelous video technician I have ever worked with in my entire life.' Hey! Earth to Jeffrey! What's going on in that gorgeous but utterly complex head of yours?"

"I was just thinking that sometimes, tapes *do* lie."

The train seemed to be slowing. "One more minute on this rattletrap and I'll die of thirst," Scott said aloud to the empty freight car. "Not to mention hunger." He glanced out the partly opened door of the car, checking up and down the tracks. It was all clear.

He slung the duffel bag over his shoulder and waited until the train's speed was slow enough. Then he leaped gracefully from the car, imagining himself as some sort of large, ferocious jungle cat, power surging through his supple body. He landed in an easy roll along the side of the tracks, righted himself quickly, and slunk behind a stack of crates to get his bearings.

"So where am I?" he asked under his breath. Obviously he was in a small town, the kind of western settlement that looked like a ghost town. The cars parked along the dusty street had Arizona license plates. He knew enough about the country and the railroad routes to recognize his location almost immediately.

"Good old Sangwav, Arizona," he decided aloud. He chuckled. "Sangwav—the Paiute word for sin."

He peered down the dark street until he made out the lighted windows of a bar he'd been in once before. "Speaking of sin, it's time to get myself a little liquid refreshment."

A few minutes later, he was in the dingy bar. He ordered a cold beer and sat drinking it, surrounded by other barflies who preferred getting soused in a seedy joint to drinking champagne at a real New Year's Eve party. The late news was just coming on the television set.

"The FBI and police departments in three states are still searching for eighteen-year-old college students Jessica and Elizabeth Wakefield," said the reporter. Scott nodded, impressed that the twins had kept ahead of the police for so long already. "Jessica Wakefield has been identified as the young woman who appeared on a surveillance video at the scene of a store holdup near Moapa, Nevada, early this morning," the reporter continued. "With the death this afternoon of a twenty-year-old clerk who was shot in the incident, the charge has been upped to murder in the first degree."

A satisfied smirk spread across Scott's face. Sooner or later, the cops would catch up to the pretty little Wakefield twins. And when they did, they'd spend days interrogating them, confident

168

that they had their suspect in custody. By the time they realized their error, Scott would be in Mexico.

"This just in," the reporter said suddenly, a look of surprise on her face as somebody handed her a slip of paper. "Nevada state police say that a third suspect is being sought in connection with this morning's murder. The suspect is a Caucasian male in his twenties. He is approximately five foot nine inches tall, with light brown hair. No positive identification has been made."

Scott felt his face growing red with outrage. Somehow, somebody had seen him. He chugged his beer, keeping his eyes on the screen. But the newscaster had nothing else to report about the case. Scott forced himself to take slow, deep breaths. If he lost his temper now, he would only draw attention to himself.

He couldn't believe it. After all his successful efforts to keep anyone from linking him to his crimes, those silly little teenagers had blown it for him. Because of them, he'd been forced to rob that store near Moapa. Now somebody could connect him with a crime. And the charge was first-degree murder.

Scott slammed two dollars down on the bar and stalked out the door.

"Dammit, I'm a suspect," he muttered, keeping his voice low enough not to be heard above the sound of his own boots on the board sidewalks. He had to think quickly. He had to determine his next step. And he had to do it before anyone noticed how closely he fit the description of the police's third murder suspect.

Scott took another deep breath. Maybe he still had a chance. The description on the news was a sketchy one. Without a witness who could place him at the murder scene, the description wouldn't be enough grounds for the police to hold him. *A witness*.

"There are only two people alive who can positively identify me from that murder scene—Jessica and Elizabeth," Scott whispered. "I should have followed my instincts and killed them."

The image of Jessica's pretty face and parted lips in the moonlight washed over his brain. Scott shook his head. This was no time to get sentimental. He'd gotten sentimental when he got to know Jessica in the first place. He'd been thinking with his hormones instead of his brains. But it wouldn't happen again.

"I never should have left any witnesses alive—blondes or not," he reprimanded himself. "Well, there won't be any witnesses alive for long. I'll find Jessica and Elizabeth Wakefield before the FBI does. And I'll make absolutely certain that they don't talk. Ever."

He stomped down the dark, chilly street toward the town's one motel. The only noise was the wind whistling through the piñon trees and the hollow echo of his boot heels against dry wood.

Chapter
Nine

Fran and the others had gone, and Jeff was alone in the FBI field office. He had decided to remain in Nevada through the night, in hopes that the new information he'd put out over the wire might get him a new lead—on either the twins or the mysterious man behind Jessica. He hated sitting at a desk while the black Jeep moved farther and farther away from him. But all in all, it made sense to wait until he knew where he was going before he set out to get there.

It had been a long day. In one corner of the mostly darkened office, a green-shaded desk lamp cast a yellow circle of light over the metal surface of Jeff's desk. In its glow, Jeff slept fitfully, his head resting on a stack of police reports on armed robberies throughout Nevada.

Jessica Wakefield was with him, wearing the Stetson hat. And her long blond hair caressed his arm as she leaned in to whisper something in his ear. She was trying to tell him something, to give him some clue to solving a very important mystery. But as hard as he tried, he couldn't understand what she was saying. A loud, insistent clamoring filled his ears, blocking the sound of her lovely voice.

Jeff awoke with a start. Inches from his head, the telephone rang insistently.

"Jeff, it's Keisha, calling from the airport in Denver. Sorry to bother you so late."

Jeff shook his head, trying to get his bearings. "How late is it?" he asked groggily.

"Almost midnight, Nevada time. I have news, Jeff. The agents here told me as soon as I got off the plane. Earlier tonight, three local police officers in a small town near Diamond Butte chased the Wakefield twins."

"Why wasn't I informed?"

"I don't know. I guess they thought we'd moved our center of operations to Colorado. Apparently the local police in Arizona called our Denver office with it."

"When did it happen?"

"Hours ago, but Denver just got the word. Anyhow, the Wakefields drove off in a black Jeep and somehow managed to elude the officers."

Jeff's eyes shot open. "Are you sure it was the Wakefields?"

"The girls they saw sure fit the description.

And the Jeep had the right license plate number."

"How the heck did they manage to get away?"

"Search me. The officers were pretty chagrined about it. They even fired several shots, but they couldn't stop the kids. You've got to hand it to those twins—"

"The police fired at them? My God, Keish, these girls are only eighteen years old!"

Keisha sighed. "Don't go getting sentimental on us, Jeff, just because they happen to be knock-outs. From what I've heard, the police acted in accordance with policy."

"I don't give a flying leap about policy. I'm worried about two eighteen-year-old kids!"

"Eighteen is plenty old enough to put the officers and the community in jeopardy. The all-points bulletin does say they're armed and dangerous."

"Yeah, but I also know these girls! And I'm telling you—it's a bum rap. You must have heard about the man standing behind Jessica on that videotape. I'm convinced that he's the key."

"I've heard enough of your wild hunches to know they usually pan out. But you can't ask every law-enforcement official in three states to ignore policy and risk people's lives based on your intuition."

"I know," Jeff said, resigned.

"Until we know more about this mystery man of yours, we have to consider Jessica Wakefield as our number-one murder suspect."

"I just wish I knew where the twins were heading—and if the man in the shadows is still with them. If I could get to them before the police do, I might be able to find some answers."

"We're doing our best, Jeff."

"I know you are, Keish. But I'd like to find those girls before this thing escalates into another OK Corral."

"Believe me, we're trying. We've got a massive search going on in Arizona, even through the night."

"But Arizona's a big state, and a lot of the northern region is remote. It will be next to impossible to find them if we have to rely on hit-or-miss search tactics."

"We may not have anything else to go on," Keisha reminded him. "That run-in with the cops was hours ago. They could be anywhere by now."

"Have you tried calling Steven Wakefield back? Maybe they've checked in with him."

"I tried. They haven't."

Jeff snapped his fingers. "Tom Watts!" he said suddenly. "I don't know why I didn't think of it before. They were on their way to Vail to meet him. Maybe Elizabeth will try to call him at his hotel room there."

"Maybe, but it sounds as if he isn't likely to cooperate with us—even if he does hear from Elizabeth. What makes you think he'd tell you if she did try to reach him?"

"I'm certain he wouldn't. But we don't have to rely on Tom's goodwill toward the Bureau. We have enough evidence to order a wiretap on his phone." He shook his head. "I hate to do that, though."

"We've got probable cause," Keisha reminded him. "And I don't see a better way to get a lead on Elizabeth's current location."

"All right. Have it set up as soon as you arrive in Vail," Jeff said. "Also, I've decided it's time to move my own operations. This case has moved out of Nevada. I'm not doing any good here, and I can't see much use in wandering blindly around the Arizona mesas."

"Does that mean you'll be joining me here in Colorado?"

"Yes. Tom's our only solid lead on this thing so far. I want to talk to him in person."

"Should I wait for you in Denver, and we'll go on to Vail together?"

"No," Jeff decided. "I'll take a chopper straight into Vail. It'll be a lot faster. I have to figure out where those girls are before the local yokels find them first and blow them away."

Jeff stopped, imagining three small-town police officers firing at an innocent and unarmed Jessica Wakefield.

Her blond hair swung out under her Stetson hat as she whirled, terrified at the sound of their shouts. She froze, her blue-green eyes wide at the sight of their weapons. Fire flashed from the steel barrels. And Jessica's slender form crumpled, a crimson stain spreading across her college T-shirt.

Then, in Jeff's mind, he was identifying Jessica's body at the morgue. The vision reminded him of another rainy night at the morgue and another woman's bullet-ravaged body. Summer.

"Jeff? Is everything all right?" Keisha's voice held a note of concern.

Jeff blinked, and the vision was gone. "Yeah. Everything's fine. What did you say?"

"I said, happy New Year."

Jeff looked at his watch. Sure enough, it was the first day of January—the first day of a new year. It was supposed to be a time of celebration, filled with joyful expectations for the future. Jeff stared at the photographs of Jessica and Summer, and all he could feel was despair.

"What a rotten way to begin the new year," Jessica grumbled, slouched in the front seat of the Jeep.

The twins had stopped to catch some sleep, but only for a couple hours. Now a red-eyed Elizabeth was driving the Jeep along a one-lane paved road, through a dim landscape of lumpy rock formations and patches of snow. Shades of peach and terracotta were beginning to tint their night-grayed surfaces, hinting of the coming sunrise. Jessica peered through the dirt on the windshield at the pink-tinged sky ahead. They were still traveling east.

"There is not a house, or a town, or another car anywhere—not to mention a gas station!" she said. "How are we on gas?"

"The tank is almost as empty as we are," Elizabeth said in a strained voice, not looking at Jessica.

"Well, my New Year's resolution is to stay close to civilization at all times—unless I'm carrying a week's worth of chocolate-chip cookies and a whole case of soda."

Elizabeth glared at her. "I can think of a few better New Year's resolutions for you," she snapped. "How about resolving to show some good judgment, for a change? How about resolving not to do idiotic things like sharing our Jeep and our room with strange men? How about resolving to use your brain instead of your glands when you meet a guy?"

"I can tell you got up on the wrong side of the Jeep," Jessica said. "You can't blame me for everything. I—" Something under the hood started to clang, and Jessica could feel the Jeep losing power.

"Oh, God, no!" Elizabeth wailed. The Jeep began to limp toward the side of the road.

"Is it busted?" Jessica asked. "We can't be out of gas!"

"Why not?"

"You heard the radio report last time we were

close enough to the civilized world to get one. The cops are on our trail! We have to keep this Jeep moving!"

"The only way we'll do that is if you get out and push," Elizabeth said over her shoulder as she jumped out to check the engine. "This thing isn't going another inch. We'll have to walk."

"Walk? But I can't carry all my suitcases! I'll have to leave behind my best party clothes!"

Elizabeth whirled on her. "How dare you worry about your clothes when we're in such a mess! You are the most immature, self-centered person—"

"Don't yell at me! I'm in the same mess you're in!" Jessica shot back. Both twins grabbed some warm clothing and their backpacks from the backseat of the Jeep and began hurrying along the road, toward a pale sunrise that seemed to give off no heat. "And what gives you the right to call me immature?" Jessica continued. "Are you going to pull your four-minutes-older thing again?"

"It has nothing to do with those four lousy minutes! It has to do with your four lousy IQ points! You're the one who took up with Scott in the first place!

"No way am I going to listen to the it's-all-Jessica's-fault routine again. What's wrong, Liz? Are you incapable of making your own decisions? It was my idea to give Scott a ride. But nobody forced you to agree. Nobody held a gun to your head. . . ."

Jessica stopped, realizing what she had said. She stared at Elizabeth for a moment, shaken. Then she turned away. The twins walked on in silence. They had covered a quarter-mile when another realization hit Jessica. She swung her backpack around her shoulder as she walked and began to paw frantically through it.

"What is it now?" Elizabeth asked. "Did you forget to take your hairbrush?"

"This is serious," Jessica hissed. "I forgot my wallet. We'll have to go back for it." She turned back toward the Jeep, still visible in the distance. Elizabeth grabbed her arm.

"There's no time, Jess. We have to keep moving."

"But, Liz, all my money is in that wallet! Without it, we're nearly broke! If I know you, you're carrying traveler's checks instead of cash."

"Of course I'm carrying traveler's checks," Elizabeth replied, a note of acid lacing her usual infuriating, more-reasonable-than-thou voice. "No normal person goes on a vacation with hundreds of dollars in cash. What if it got stolen? Or what if some fool left it in the Jeep?"

"And what if our names were plastered all over every newspaper in the state, so that the first clerk who saw 'Wakefield' on a traveler's check would have the cops on our backs in an instant?"

181

Elizabeth's shoulders slumped. "You're right," she said tearfully. "If our name isn't in the newspapers yet, it will be soon."

"So we can't risk using your traveler's checks. We have to get my wallet. It's not that far—"

An approaching siren wailed, somewhere in the grayness to the west. Jessica saw her own fear reflected in her sister's face. "Run for those rocks!" Jessica yelled.

The twins scrambled behind an outcropping of mauve sandstone just before flashing lights appeared on the road, against the western horizon. Within a minute, three state police cars had skidded to a stop near the black Jeep. Uniformed officers leaped from the cars and surrounded the Jeep, assault rifles aimed and ready. After a moment, they must have determined that the twins had left the scene. They swarmed around the Jeep, obviously intent on tearing it apart to search for clues. From a distance Jessica watched as one of the state troopers lifted something from the backseat.

"The Stetson," Jessica whispered, recognizing Scott's hat. A sudden emptiness yawned in her chest. Never again would she fall for a guy she'd just met, Jessica vowed. She remembered standing in the poolside gazebo at Caesars Palace. She could feel and smell Scott's hat on her head and his arms on her back as she tasted the sweetness of a magical, moonlit kiss.

Her sister's hand tightened, viselike, on her

arm, catapulting Jessica back to the present. Elizabeth's eyes were wide with fright. "Come on, Liz," Jessica said into her ear. "The cops haven't seen us. Let's get away while there's still time."

Elizabeth nodded as if she'd just woken up. "Right," she said. "We should stick to the rocks for cover but keep moving parallel to the road."

"I wish we'd thought to bring the map from the Jeep," Jessica said.

"Me too. But I remember a town just a few miles ahead. We can get some supplies there, if we can disguise ourselves enough to keep people from recognizing us."

"What town?" Jessica asked, though she didn't know why it mattered.

"Oh, I don't remember. It had a funny name. Uh . . . I know! It's called Sangwav."

Scott hid his face in a copy of the *Sangwav Weekly Courier* and sipped his coffee while he listened to the breakfast conversation in the next booth of the diner. He'd chosen his seat carefully, positioning himself with his back to the two local police officers who sat at the adjacent table.

In addition, he had a good view of the street from his booth, while his face was hidden by a red-checkered curtain. He looked across the street toward the adobe building that was the town's general store. Not surprisingly, business at both establishments was slow; it was seven o'clock on the morning after New Year's Eve. Most of the town was sleeping off the effects of the night before, oblivious to the forces that were about to converge on Sangwav.

Scott grinned behind his newspaper. The Wakefield twins were coming. And if Scott had his way, neither Wakefield would survive the day. He was sure the twins would show up in Sangwav; he knew the back roads in this part of the state as well as he knew his own mother. There were only two roads Jessica and Elizabeth could have ended up on. And those roads met smack dab in the middle of downtown metropolitan Sangwav.

All Scott needed to know now was when to expect the girls. And the police were his best bet for that kind of information—especially when they were off their guard, eating doughnuts, drinking orange juice, and talking shop. Unfortunately, the town drunk's New Year's Eve antics were not of particular interest to Scott.

Scott suddenly noticed Jessica's eyes staring at him from the newspaper page he held in front of his face. It was the still photograph from the surveillance camera at the store near Moapa. She looked terrified, he thought. And betrayed. Her gaze caused a strange reaction in Scott. A familiar, pleasant feeling of omnipotence surged through his body at the knowledge of his power over another person. But his pride was tinged by longing and sorrow. Jessica was a cute kid who had really liked him. And that moonlit kiss by the pool at Caesars had been something special.

That doesn't matter now, he told himself. If Jessica had the chance, Scott knew she'd turn him over to the police in an instant. Well, Jessica wasn't going to get that chance.

"So the two gals are heading this way, Andy?" the thin, nervous-sounding rookie asked.

"That's what the reports say," drawled the older officer, a heavyset man with a deep, pleasant voice. "They'll probably be in the vicinity sometime in the next few hours. State troopers found their car just before sunrise. It was on the western road, a few miles out of town."

"A Jeep, wasn't it?"

"That's right. With a whole lot of stuff inside, mostly women's clothes. It belongs to the Wakefield twins, all right. It's a two-year-old black Wrangler, like the all-points bulletin said."

The conversation paused while the nervous young cop took a bite of his doughnut. "What about the male accomplice?" he asked a minute later. "Any sign of him?"

"Nah. There were no men's clothes in that Jeep—only the cowboy hat the girl was wearing in the video. I hear the FBI is all het up about finding the dude. But I can't see how it makes much sense to spend time on him."

"You're right about that. I mean, lots of guys

185

are short with light brown hair. Does the FBI have any clue as to his whereabouts?"

"The FBI doesn't know squat. They ain't even put a name to him yet. I say we forget about him and watch for the twins instead. Two pretty little girls like that are gonna stand out in this town like a peacock in the desert—if they're dumb enough to come into town, that is. The state troopers are betting they'll stick to the surrounding country-side. These girls are experienced fugitives; they probably have hideouts with caches of supplies all over those canyons."

"You think they're as dangerous as everyone says?" asked the young officer. "I hear they've got an arsenal of weapons and have murdered more than a dozen people. But gosh, Andy, the one on that tape sure didn't look like a killer."

"You never can tell," Andy warned. "Those girls are listed as armed and dangerous, so we should be ready to use any force necessary to stop them. The FBI wants them alive, though—Bureau wants to question them about that male accomplice of theirs."

"Not on your life," Scott whispered, staring at the photograph in the newspaper. The FBI would never get the chance to question the Wakefields about him. He would find Jessica and Elizabeth before the police did. And he would use any force necessary to stop the twins—permanently.

*　　*　　*

Trudging over the rocky terrain was strenuous, but Elizabeth knew that walking on the road was too risky. Instead, she steered her sister on a course that ran parallel to it, watching for occasional glimpses of the pavement through the rocky formations that rose from the otherwise desertlike plateau. The early-morning air was chilly. But after more than an hour of walking, Elizabeth had worked up an uncomfortable sweat in her down vest and sweater. She sighed. "Maybe we should have left the ski clothes in the Jeep."

Jessica skirted a patch of snow. "I don't know. As soon as we stop walking, I'm sure we'll feel the cold again."

"I feel like we'll never stop walking. Do you think the police have picked up our trail?"

"I doubt it. They're faster than we are, and they know the area. If they were on to us, I think we'd see them by now." She stifled a yawn. "What about this Sackwack town you said we were close to? Could we have missed it?"

"Sangwav," Elizabeth corrected. "I don't think we missed it. If I remember correctly, this road runs right through the center of it. But I could be wrong. I don't have a map for a brain."

Jessica opened her mouth as if she were about to make a sarcastic comment. But a glare from Elizabeth snapped it shut.

"I wish we could stop and sleep," Elizabeth said. "But we don't have time. We need a telephone so I can call Tom. He and the others must be worried sick about us."

"I think I'd rather have food than a telephone."

"It's more important for us to get water," Elizabeth said.

Jessica sighed. "How? By now, everyone on the planet and several neighboring star systems has seen that video of me holding up a store. It's hard enough for one blond teenage stranger to be invisible. It'll be impossible for two of us!"

Elizabeth stopped walking suddenly. She shielded her eyes to peer ahead into the sunrise, which was opening across the sky like a flower, in delicate shades of lavender and apricot.

"What is it, Liz? Cops?"

Elizabeth shook her head. The sun's first brilliant rays were shooting up from the horizon, obscuring her vision. But up ahead, something ghostly was rising from the stark landscape. She shook her head again and began picking her way up a sagebrush-dotted incline. "It must have been a mirage."

"What must have been a mirage?"

"I thought I saw something shining up ahead. I think the sun is playing tricks on my eyes. Anyhow, we need to disguise ourselves somehow. I have my sunglasses in my backpack. Do you have yours with you?"

"No, I left them in the Jeep. But I do have a

silk scarf. It will look kind of stupid with a ski jacket, but at least it'll cover my hair."

"Good. I've got a ski cap. I'll put my hair up and tuck it under. That's all we can do for now. When we get to the town, we'll try to buy you a better disguise."

Jessica pulled out a compact and inspected her face. "Actually, I think I'm safe," she said. "Nobody will recognize me—I've never looked this awful in my life! I was thinking that *you* had dark circles under your eyes. I guess they don't call us mirror images for nothing."

The twins walked on in silence for a few minutes. "There's my mirage again," Elizabeth said, pointing. "It looks like a town or a castle or something."

Jessica squinted toward the sunrise. Then her eyes widened. "Elizabeth, that's no mirage! I think we've found Sagwag!"

"Sangwav," Elizabeth corrected automatically. But for the first time in hours, she felt her spirits rising. Jessica's eyes filled with tears of relief.

By the time they finally reached the town, the sun was up. Elizabeth's watch said it was eight thirty in the morning. She tucked a stray lock of hair under her wool ski cap and crossed her fingers as the twins stepped out onto the main road.

"Let's just pray that a store will be open so early on New Year's Day," she said.

"Yeah, and that the Arizona state police department isn't planning to throw us a welcome-to-Sangwav party," Jessica added.

They walked quickly along the main street. Elizabeth felt horribly conspicuous in the early-morning glare.

"There's a general store," Jessica said excitedly, pointing to an adobe building. "See it? It's right across the street from that diner with the tacky sign. Come on!" She almost broke into a run, but Elizabeth pulled her back.

"Not so fast!" Elizabeth said. "We don't want to be noticed, remember? Stay cool and be careful of what you tell people. Remember—if you have to say anything, tell them our car broke down on the way to the Grand Canyon."

"Okay, okay. Can we go in, already?"

"Not yet. We have to case the place first. You wait around the corner, and I'll check out the inside of the store. You look around the street."

"What am I looking for?"

"Anything." Elizabeth pretended to read a nearby movie poster while actually scanning the small store through the window. "It's clear inside," she pronounced after a moment. "No TVs and no surveillance cameras. Two clerks at the counter—a young guy and an older woman reading a newspaper. There aren't any customers. And the phone's right next to the entrance."

"I just hope they've got food. I'm dying of hunger."

"Don't think about that now," Elizabeth hissed. "Does the neighborhood seem safe? Did you see any police cars?"

"Nope. Only a green convertible parked on the side street. The other cars are all boring."

"Have you seen any people around? Anyone who might have spotted us?"

"I think somebody came out of that diner a second ago—I saw him out of the corner of my eye. But he must have turned down the side street. Don't worry. If he were a cop, we'd know it by now. We're safe."

Elizabeth took a deep breath and saw Jessica doing the same. Then the twins sauntered into the store, trying to look like hikers.

Elizabeth reached the pay phone and tried to look nonchalant as she scrambled in her backpack for the telephone number of the hotel in Vail. Her hands were shaking uncontrollably. Suddenly the exhaustion and fear of the last day overwhelmed her. She had to blink back tears. At the same time, she noticed Jessica's casual facade crumble into a mad dash toward the junk-food aisle.

Tom will make everything all right, Elizabeth promised herself as the phone in Tom's room began to ring. "Please pick up!" she whispered into the receiver. "Please, please, please pick up the phone!"

*　　*　　*

"Would you like paper or plastic bags?" the store clerk asked Jessica as she dumped her armload of items on the counter. She'd found bottles of mineral water, two boxes of cookies, a half-dozen bagels, a baseball cap, and a pair of dark glasses.

In her scramble to collect all the supplies she could carry, Jessica hadn't even noticed the young clerk. Now she looked up abruptly—and gazed into the warmest brown eyes she had ever seen. One look into those brown eyes melted Jessica's resolve to control her infatuation for guys she knew nothing about. And it wasn't only his eyes. The rest of his face was cute, too, she decided. He had black hair, high cheekbones, and a deep cleft in his chin. And his navy-and-green rugby shirt set off his broad shoulders admirably. The clerk's name tag said *Rick*.

Jessica smiled shyly. "Paper or plastic?" she asked. "Well, what would you recommend, Rick?" She noticed that the gray-haired woman looked up from her newspaper to observe the exchange. *Another overprotective mother who thinks no girl is good enough for her little prince*, she thought.

"That depends," Rick responded with a grin that made Jessica feel as if she could walk another ten miles through the canyons if he were at the end of the road. "Paper holds more," he continued.

"But plastic is easier to carry long distances. Are you going far?"

I'm going anywhere you're going, honey, she wanted to say. Instead, she smiled. "Yes, a long, long way," she said. "We're hikers. I bet a strong guy like you does a lot of hiking."

"Oh, I do a little." He leaned forward on the counter. "But I'm more into driving. I'm restoring a 1966 T-bird convertible. I've still got a little cosmetic work to do on the outside—and the top's broken, so I can't put it up. But what's inside is the important part. I've got an awesome new engine in her, and she rides like a dream!"

Jessica made her voice breathy. "I love convertibles, even in the winter! And 1966 was definitely the best year for them," she added, though she didn't have the faintest idea what she was talking about.

"This baby's a real classic. In fact, you two have a lot in common," he said with a slight rise of his eyebrows. "Good looks, clean lines, and a whole lot of style."

"I noticed it parked outside," Jessica replied. "It sure looks fast! I knew it had to be yours the minute I laid eyes on you." Suddenly she remembered that she had hardly slept in twenty-four hours and wasn't wearing any makeup, and she wanted to sink into the floor. But Rick didn't seem to mind her appearance. In fact, he couldn't take his eyes off her as he rang up her purchases.

Maybe guys from rugged places like this prefer the natural look.

An abrupt movement behind him grabbed Jessica's attention. Rick's mother had just turned the page of her newspaper and then sat up straight in her chair, her brown eyes widening. Jessica pretended not to notice as the woman examined Jessica's face and then looked back at her newspaper—once, twice, and then a third time. Then her gaze shifted to Elizabeth.

"They're bagged," Rick said cheerfully, gesturing toward her groceries.

"We certainly are," Jessica said as Rick's mother stepped through a doorway into an adjacent office. As the woman moved, Jessica caught a glimpse of the word *Wakefield* in heavy type, near the photo of herself in Scott's Stetson hat.

"What do you mean?" Rick asked.

"Nothing," Jessica said, thinking fast. Through the partly opened doorway she could see Rick's mother dialing a telephone. Then words began tumbling out of Jessica's mouth before she knew what she was going to say. "Rick, we're in real trouble. Our car broke down a couple miles from town, and my sist—uh, my friend—left her wallet on the front seat. I know it's a lot to ask, but she's awfully worried about it. Could we borrow your car to drive back for it?"

Rick held out the keys. "Only if you promise to let me buy you dinner tonight."

"Sure thing!" Jessica grabbed the keys, scooped up the plastic grocery bags, and raced for the door.

Elizabeth tapped her foot impatiently as Tom's phone rang for the eighth time. *He must have fallen asleep after being up all night worrying about me.* "Wake up, Tom!" she ordered aloud. "Answer the phone!"

Finally he picked up the receiver. At the same time, Elizabeth saw something through the window and froze. A police cruiser had just glided into view at the other end of the street. "Tom, it's me!" she stammered into the phone. "I—we—"

She stifled a cry as someone grabbed her arm and began dragging her out the door. It was Jessica, loaded down with groceries and dangling a set of car keys. Elizabeth wondered how in the world Jessica had found them a car, but there was no time to ask. She scrambled after her sister, leaving the telephone receiver swinging at the end of its cord.

Without opening the car door, Jessica catapulted herself into the green T-bird convertible they had seen earlier. Groceries skittered across the front seat like popcorn.

"Where are we going?" Elizabeth screamed as she opened the other door and clambered in, shoving aside a box of cookies.

Jessica gunned the engine. "Does it matter?"

Luckily the car was facing away from the town's main thoroughfare—and away from the approaching police car. Elizabeth was hurled back against the upholstery as the T-bird lurched out of the parking space and fled Sangwav, Arizona. A moment later, a siren began to scream somewhere behind them.

Chapter Ten

Tom felt warm and comfortable. But deep in his mind, he knew that something was wrong with Elizabeth. He couldn't remember exactly what he was worried about; it would be easier to think if that incessant ringing would stop.

Ringing? His body went rigid. The telephone was ringing. *Elizabeth!* Tom fought his way through the bedspread that was wrapped around his fully dressed body. He hadn't meant to fall asleep. Danny and Isabella had gone to the New Year's Eve party without him, and Tom had waited up in front of the TV, hoping for news of the twins. As he fumbled for the phone, he glanced at his roommate's empty bed. *Danny must be in Isabella's room,* Tom decided.

"Elizabeth?" he yelled into the phone.

"Tom, it's me!" Elizabeth stammered. Her voice shook with fear and exhaustion. Something was terribly wrong.

"Liz, what is it?"

"I—we—" Then she uttered a wordless cry, which was cut short.

"Elizabeth? Elizabeth! Please answer me, Liz. What's the matter? Where are you?"

There was only silence.

Tom felt as if he were going into shock. He forced himself to breathe deeply and to think. Silence on the other end of the line meant no dial tone. And no dial tone meant that the telephone Elizabeth had called from was still off the hook. But where was that telephone? Where was Elizabeth?

As a reporter, Tom knew how to get his hands on information he needed. Now those instincts took over. He would trace the call, he decided, staring at the receiver. He had a friend at the telephone company in California. She had helped out on past stories; he was sure he could persuade her to run a quick trace. But a call couldn't be traced unless both ends stayed off the hook. He snapped his fingers. "Isabella's phone!" He laid the receiver on the bed and scrambled across the hall to pound on his friend's door.

"It's Tom!" he called. "Let me in. It's an emergency!"

Danny pulled open the door, wearing pajama bottoms and no shirt. "What's wrong? Have you heard something from the twins?"

Tom was already running to the telephone.

"What is it?" Isabella asked sleepily, emerging from the bathroom and tying the sash on a thick, terry-cloth bathrobe.

Tom ignored them. His friend at the phone company was picking up. "Sara! This is Tom. I need you to trace a call for me right now. You'll have to trust me on this—there's no time to explain."

"Tom, you know I'm not supposed to—"

"It's life or death, Sara. I mean it!"

The urgency in his voice must have made an impression on her. "All right, Tom. I know you wouldn't ask if it weren't vital. But I'll expect a full explanation later."

He gave her the phone number in his hotel room. A few minutes later Sara read him a telephone number with an Arizona area code.

"Now I need you to look in your reverse directory and tell me where that number is."

"Tom! I can't—"

"Yes, you can. Please, Sara. If I was back at the television station, I could look it up for myself. This is urgent, I swear."

A minute later he threw down the phone and tore off a slip of hotel stationery. Danny and Isabella stared at him, their mouths open.

"What's going on?" Danny asked. "Did you find the twins?"

"Tell us what we can do to help," Isabella implored. Her dark eyes were wide with concern.

"Please, Tom! Jessica's my best friend!"

Tom shook his head. The FBI man said he could be held as an accomplice; he refused to involve his friends as well. "Just stay close to the phones in case the twins call again."

"Again?" Danny asked. "What are you talking—"

Tom raced back to his own room before Danny had finished the question. In his fist he clutched a slip of hotel stationery with a scrawled phone number and address on it. Elizabeth had phoned from a place called Sangwav, Arizona. He grabbed his wallet from the dresser and scooped up the keys to Danny's rented Toyota. Elizabeth was in trouble; he had to get to Sangwav.

But a woman he'd never seen before stood in the open doorway of his room, blocking his path. She was only of average height, but something about her scarlet suit and self-assured air made her seem much larger.

"Tom Watts?" she asked.

"Yes, but I'm on my way out right now. I—"

"You certainly are. You're coming with us, Mr. Watts. I'm Special Agent Keisha Williamson of the Federal Bureau of Investigation, Nevada office." She introduced two men who stood behind her. Both were agents from the Colorado office. "My colleagues and I have some questions for you."

"I told you, I—"

"And I told you to come with us," she commanded. Her hand moved to her hip, parting her red blazer just enough to reveal a semiautomatic pistol in a shoulder holster. Her colleagues glared at Tom threateningly, each resting a hand on his own weapon. Tom sighed, his eyes on the guns. Then he stepped into the hallway behind Agent Williamson. The other agents followed. As he passed their room, Tom saw Danny and Isabella peering out. He shook his head slightly at them, and they retreated.

"Where are we going?" he asked Agent Williamson, who was obviously in charge.

"We have a temporary field office set up in the basement of the resort," she answered. "We're taking you there for questioning."

"What do you want from me?"

"Answers. We know you just spoke with Elizabeth Wakefield. We want to know where she is."

"How should I know where she is?" Tom demanded. "You're the FBI, not me."

"Don't get smart, kid," snarled the tallest and broadest of the two other agents. "Or we can make your life real miserable."

Tom grimaced. This guy sounded like something out of a gangster movie. Unfortunately, he was built like something out of a Godzilla movie. Tom had been a star football player at Sweet Valley University the year before, but he knew he was no match for the brawny FBI operative—

Bruce somebody, Keisha had called him. Mentally, Tom dubbed him Agent Brute. But he addressed his comments to Keisha. "If you were bugging my phone—and I assume you were—you must know that Elizabeth didn't tell me anything. Why didn't you just trace the call?"

The agent stopped in front of the elevator and inspected her flat-heeled red pumps. Suddenly she didn't seem so intimidating. "We tried," she admitted. "We had an equipment malfunction."

Tom struggled to keep his smirk to himself. He knew where Elizabeth was—or had been a few minutes earlier. The FBI didn't know. If he could only escape from Keisha Williamson and her goons, he might be able to reach the twins before the FBI and the police did. The armed-robbery and murder charges against Jessica were a gross mistake. But only now was he realizing just how badly the situation had ballooned. It had expanded to include wiretaps, threats, and a network of FBI agents across at least three states. And he was afraid that sooner or later, it would explode in Elizabeth and Jessica's faces.

Jeff sat in a roomful of computers, recording devices, and telecommunications equipment, cursing his luck. "Hundreds of thousands of dollars of state-of-the-art equipment and you tell me we had an equipment malfunction?" he asked a frightened-looking engineer. "What the hell went wrong?"

"A simple power fluctuation interrupted the trace," the young man admitted, clicking on a mouse to pull up a screen full of complex data on one of the computers. "I guess the room wasn't wired to handle so much current."

Jeff clenched his teeth and forced his voice to stay quiet. "All right. See what you can do about making sure it goes through next time—though I doubt we'll have a next time."

He ran a hand through his thick brown hair. It galled him to know that he'd blown the chance to pinpoint Elizabeth's location. But two other possible sources of information remained. Maybe someone would call in from Arizona with news that an agent or cop had spotted the twins. Or maybe Jeff could convince Tom Watts to tell him something useful about Elizabeth's whereabouts. Jeff was sure Tom didn't know her exact location; he'd been listening in on the phone call. But he might know something about her trip that would give Jeff a clue.

He looked up at the sound of a key in the lock. Keisha strolled into the room, looking beautiful and formidable in a red power suit. She held a reluctant-looking young man by the arm and was followed by the two agents sent in from the Denver office.

Jeff appraised Tom Watts silently. Tom looked about twenty years old, Jeff decided. He was as tall and wide shouldered as Jeff himself. But Jeff had a broad, powerful build; Tom was as lean and supple as a snake. He had the body of a college quarterback, Jeff realized. But that was to be expected. The dossier he'd compiled on Tom revealed that he'd been one of the best quarterbacks in California before giving up the game.

"This place looks like something out of *The Man from UNCLE*," Tom said. He spoke lightly, but his eyes glittered almost black with anger and worry. "What happens next? Let me guess. You're going to pull a retractable electric cattle prod out of your shirt button and torture me with it if I don't talk."

"I'm Jeff Marks," Jeff said, ignoring Tom's sarcasm. "We spoke on the phone last night. I know you're concerned about Elizabeth and her sister. Believe me, the best way to help them is to help us. I want you to tell me everything you know about their trip."

"Even if I knew anything," Tom asked quietly, "why would I betray my girlfriend by telling you?"

One of the Colorado agents stepped forward. The man—Bruce somebody—was so big and grim faced that he made Tom and Jeff look like Tom and Jerry. "You'll tell us because we say so," Bruce said in a threatening tone. Jeff considered silencing him, but he decided against it. A little harmless intimidation just might loosen Tom's tongue.

The young engineer didn't know that the intimidation was harmless. He eyed the big man warily. Then he quietly stood up from his computer, trembling, and left the room.

"And if you don't tell us what we want to hear," Bruce continued, staring steadily at Tom, "there's a cell in federal prison with your name on it. Have you ever heard of obstruction of justice? What about aiding and abetting a criminal?"

Tom moved so quickly that Jeff didn't have time to react. Not missing a beat, Tom slipped between the two Denver agents and out the door, which the young engineer had left slightly open.

The four FBI agents looked at one another, aghast.

"Stop or I'll shoot!" Bruce yelled, his weapon raised. But Tom was gone, veering to the right as he disappeared out the door. After a moment of confusion, all four agents scrambled into the hallway in pursuit.

Tom skidded from the corridor into a broom closet, which was directly to the right of the FBI's surveillance room. If his hunch was correct, the agents would come charging out the door and head down the hall. They would assume he had gone past the closet—they would think he had turned the corner and was fleeing toward the stairs at the end of the next hall.

Sure enough, as Tom peered through a low grate in the door, the four agents tore out of the office and rushed past the broom closet, their guns thrust before them. As soon as they had rounded the bend, he slipped out the door and headed in the opposite direction, into the underground garage. Luckily the rented Toyota was in Danny's name. If Tom's name were attached to it, he knew, the FBI surely would have taken steps to cut off his access.

Escape felt like his only option. He loved Elizabeth. He refused to betray her. He didn't know what had happened or how Jessica had ended up on television apparently robbing a store at gunpoint. But he did know where Elizabeth had called from, and he was determined to make it there himself.

He wondered what else he might know that the FBI would be able to use. Well, he knew that Jessica, in her usual harebrained way, had convinced Elizabeth to ignore her own better judgment. He knew they had picked up a hitchhiker named Scott something. Thunderstruck, Tom almost stopped the car.

"Why didn't I think of that?" he asked himself aloud. "Obviously this Scott guy is the key to it all!" Frantically he tried to remember Scott's last name. Even if Elizabeth had been right and the guy was a med student, better with a cadaver than a car engine, this Scott might know where they were or what had happened along the way. Or what kind of danger they might be in right now.

In his mind, Tom replayed the abrupt end to

Elizabeth's last phone call. Once more, he heard her halting voice and her aborted scream. He vowed to find her while there was still time.

At least, he hoped there was still time.

Exhaustion, relief, and sugar had affected Jessica's mind. Oh, sure, she still had problems. In fact, she reflected, she had more problems than she could keep track of. She was still terrified that the police would spot her and Elizabeth in the green T-bird convertible. She was scared to death of Scott, but she knew Elizabeth was intent on finding him and proving their innocence. And she was shivering, since they were shooting down the road on New Year's morning in a convertible with a top that wouldn't go up.

The one other teeny-tiny problem was that she wasn't sure exactly where they were heading. Even Elizabeth, who was driving, didn't seem to know. All the twins knew about their surroundings was that the patches of snow were getting larger and the shapes of the rock formations were getting eerier—in a lumpy, mutated sort of way. In fact, the place looked like the surface of the moon.

For now, none of that mattered. Jessica was so happy to be safe and alive and free—and to have eaten half a dozen chocolate-chip cookies—that she felt positively giddy. She smiled at her sister. Despite Elizabeth's dark glasses, Jessica could tell that her identical twin was in an identical mood.

"Are you as punchy as I am?" Elizabeth asked with a giggle. In town, Elizabeth had stuffed her blond hair under a cap, but now the wind had loosened it and golden locks were whipping around her wind-chapped face.

"It must be the cookies," she announced, rounding a bend of the road in an exuberant, un-Elizabeth sort of way. "I haven't scarfed down this many cookies in months!"

"They're good for you! Too much dieting causes wrinkles," Jessica decided on the spot. "And cookie withdrawal has been shown to cause acne in laboratory rats."

"So has music withdrawal," Elizabeth said. "Turn on the radio!"

Jessica obediently switched it on and twirled the dial until she found a station. "How about Janis Joplin?" She turned up the volume, and both twins chimed in tunelessly: *"Freedom's just another word for nothing left to lose—"*

In mid-lyric, they froze. "Did you hear something?" Elizabeth asked over the music, as Janis continued to sing. Jessica nodded slowly, realizing the noise had come from behind them. But she couldn't bring herself to turn around.

A maniacal, familiar laugh exploded from the backseat. A wave of horror washed over Jessica. Elizabeth's hands were shaking so much that she could barely keep the car from swerving off the road. Scott rose like an apparition in the backseat and wrapped a muscular arm around each twin. Two days earlier, the soft hairs of his arm against the back of her neck would have sent Jessica into spasms of happiness. Now she felt only revulsion—and terror.

"Howdy, ladies!" Scott said affably. The radio was still blaring, but Jessica was afraid to move a muscle, even to turn it off. "It seems there's been a slight change of plans. The feds turned up evidence of my presence at a certain convenience store robbery yesterday morning. Seeing as how a young lady there somehow went and got herself dead, they've connected me to a first-degree-murder charge. I can't afford to do that kind of time, girls."

"We won't tell anyone you were there," Elizabeth offered in a low voice. "We'll tell them we robbed that store. Just us."

Scott's grin never reached his steel-gray eyes. "You know, girls, I would really like to trust two beautiful young women like yourselves." He shifted his arm on Jessica's back, and she felt a cold, sickening weight against her shoulder. A gun.

"I'd trade all my tomorrows for one single yesterday," Janis sang. Jessica's hand shot out of its own accord and flicked off the radio. She didn't want to give Scott any ideas. She desperately prayed for at least a few more tomorrows; yesterday had been the pits.

"If I felt for an instant that I couldn't trust the two of you to keep your mouths shut," Scott continued, "then I'd have no choice in the world but to get you somewhere real remote—and then to kill you." He laughed, playfully tousling Jessica's hair with the barrel of his gun. "And you know what, girls? I don't trust either of you—not for a second."

Chapter Eleven

"There's no time to waste!" Jeff barked at Keisha as they skidded away from the ski resort in a black FBI minivan.

"I still can't believe he got away," Keisha said, intent on the icy road. "Do you think he knows something about the twins?"

"I'm sure of it. I've radioed every agent and police cruiser in the area to be on the lookout. He couldn't have gone far. We'd have seen him by now if he were on foot, so he must have scrounged up some sort of vehicle. One thing's for sure—he's not in the hotel."

"But the state police checked. There's no record of a rental car in his name." She snapped her fingers. "I know! The roommate!"

"Of course! Why didn't we think of that sooner? His name is Danny Wyatt." Jeff flipped through a notebook. "And the other traveling companion is an Isabella Ricci," he read. "If either of those two rented a car, Tom could have borrowed it. I'll get on the radio right away and have the police check it out."

A few minutes later, the agents had their answer. Danny's rental car was a blue Toyota Corolla. And a police officer in an unmarked car had already spotted it, a mile away down the mountain road.

"Where do you think he'll go?" Keisha asked. "From what we heard on the wiretap, it sounded as if he doesn't know where the Wakefields are either."

"I have a hunch about Tom Watts. I think he knows more than he's saying. Elizabeth may not have told him her location, but I think he has some idea of where she is."

"That does make sense," Keisha said. "Why else would he have been so anxious to get away from us?"

"My guess is that he plans to make his way to Arizona, or wherever he thinks they're headed. Take the next turn, just ahead. It'll bring us to the interstate."

"You want to *drive* to Arizona? That's ridiculous, Jeff. What is it, seven hundred miles? Tom can't drive the whole way."

"He won't, if I have anything to do with it." Jeff's mouth was set in a grim, taut line. "We're going to catch up with him before he gets out of town. And we're going to make him tell us what he knows about Elizabeth and her sister."

Keisha frowned. "Jeff, you're too intense about this case. Remember, we still don't have any evidence that links the Wakefields to Summer's death."

"What about him?"

"Your man in the shadows behind Jessica?"

Jeff nodded. "*He* killed Summer—and the witnesses in all the other cases. And he killed the clerk in the Moapa store yesterday morning."

A glance showed him Keisha's expression—sympathetic, but skeptical.

"I know what you're thinking, Keish. You're going to tell me I don't have any evidence, except a blurry shot on a videotape. I'll get the evidence. But first, I'll get *him*. If we don't make it in time, he'll kill again—and soon. And I have a sick feeling that his next victims will be Jessica and Elizabeth Wakefield."

Jessica sat motionless as waves of terror washed over her body. With every jolt of the car on the snow-blanketed road, Scott's gun pressed harder against the back of her head.

"Don't slow down!" Scott growled at Elizabeth. "Not if you want your sister's pretty little head to stay in one piece."

"I can't help it," Elizabeth whispered. "There's ice on the road. It's slippery." Jessica caught her sister's tight-lipped glance and knew that Elizabeth felt as hopeless as she did. Then Elizabeth squeezed down on the accelerator and the green convertible whipped over the high, forested plateau. A stark outline of snow highlighted every branch and needle of the ponderosa and aspen trees, making them glitter, silver, in the midmorning sunlight.

Jessica began to notice buildings interspersed among the trees. Was it a town? Her mind raced, trying to think of any way to escape from Scott. Maybe they would begin to pass people, and she could attract their attention somehow. Maybe someone would notice that the man behind her held a gun to her head.

At this point, I wouldn't mind if they recognized me from the store video and called the cops to come arrest us. Anything to get her away from the whisper of Scott's breath against her neck and the pressure of his gun barrel against her head.

Then the pressure subsided, and Jessica exhaled gratefully.

Scott laughed. "Don't sound so relieved, Jess. The gun's at your shoulder. If either of you makes a move in Jacob Lake, I'll unload all six bullets into you. Got it? This town is the last outpost in the forest. After this, we hit one more dumpy village on the edge of the plateau. Then it's clear sailing all the way to the canyon. You girls ever seen the canyon?"

Despite the cold and the wind, Jessica's forehead broke out into a sweat under her baseball cap. How could he act so casual? Jessica was having trouble breathing, whether from fright or cold or the altitude, which had been climbing steadily.

Scott jabbed the gun into her shoulder. "I asked you a question, Jessica!"

"Uh—no," she stammered. "We haven't."

On the seat beside her, Elizabeth squeezed her hand. The convertible sped through the four blocks of the snow-blanketed town. Then the glittering forest enveloped the road once more. Not a single person had been outside to see them pass through. And that was the last town. The twins glanced at each other, wide-eyed with terror. Now there was no chance of help from anyone. They were on their own.

Scott smiled at the twins' wide-eyed terror. *This is better than armed robbery!* There was an odd kind of joy in manipulating people's emotions. Robbing a store never gave him more than a minute or two to lead his victims through stages of fear and hope. In a way, he felt sorry for the Wakefield girls, especially Jessica. But at the same time, he had never felt so vibrant and strong.

"You know, Jess," he said affably, "it's too bad that I'm the solitary type—and that you're such an innocent little thing. Otherwise I might have considered keeping you on, as sort of a partner in crime. Like Bonnie and Clyde. They sure had some good times."

Bonnie and Clyde. Jesse James. Billy the Kid. The role of the outlaw was one of Scott's favorites—especially when he could do it with a western, cowboy kind of flair. In the last few months, he'd perfected a few others as well. You never knew when circumstances would dictate a new identity. Sometimes he found that he couldn't remember which of his personalities was real. For instance, the moment he'd met the Wakefield twins, he'd slipped easily into one of his mental disguises. He'd known instantly which role would impress the girls. So he became an unassuming student who'd worked his way up to the University of California medical school, from a country-hick college in Montana.

The thought of Montana ruined Scott's happy mood. He pondered the aspen and ponderosa pine trees around him, their branches and needles heavy with snow and ice. "The forest near Bozeman looked a lot like this place in winter," he said suddenly, speaking more to himself than to the twins.

That northern woods had been beautiful, he recalled, in a savage, unyielding way. *Power is like that—appealing, but dangerous.* Scott remembered staring out at that dark Montana forest, longing to run between the trees and feel the icy air on his face. But he hadn't been gazing at snowy pine

216

trees from the seat of a convertible, as free as a tumbleweed in the breeze. Back then, he couldn't jump out anytime he felt like fooling around in the snow.

"Of course," he added, as if he hadn't paused at all since his last statement, "I couldn't enjoy those trees the way I can enjoy these here. I was staring at that old Montana forest from the window of a prison cell."

Until that moment, he hadn't known that Jessica and Elizabeth could possibly look any more horrified than they already did. But even the utter terror on their faces didn't cheer him up. He had spoken lightly, but Scott's thoughts were grim.

"I'm never going back," he whispered, his vow lost in the lonely whistling of the wind. "Nobody is ever going to pen me up again. I'll do anything to avoid that. Anything."

Was that a plainclothes police officer in the silver hatchback? Had he been holding a two-way radio? Tom was terrified that he would be stopped and hauled back to the ski resort. He had to make it out of town. More than that, he had to make it to Arizona. He had to find Elizabeth and Jessica before the FBI caught them. In his mind, a sickening scenario played itself out. Elizabeth stood in an Arizona desert, unarmed and defenseless, while a circle of police cars screeched to a halt around her. "Stop or we'll shoot!" shouted Agent Brute, shouldering an assault rifle.

Then a deafening roar filled the desert, and Elizabeth crumpled to the ground.

Tom shook his head to clear the image. Panic would get him nowhere. And he still had a long way to go—Arizona was seven or eight hundred miles away, he guessed. He yanked open the glove compartment and riffled through its contents. No map. He swore under his breath. All he had to do for now was get away from the resort. Once he was far from Vail and the FBI, he would stop and find a map and figure out how to get to Sangwav, Arizona.

Suddenly a black minivan swerved around a bend and appeared on the road behind him. An African-American woman was at the wheel; her companion was a large, handsome man with a thick shock of brown hair.

"Dammit!" Tom yelled, recognizing them. It was the two FBI agents, Keisha Williamson and Jeff Marks. And the minivan was quickly closing up the distance between it and Tom's blue Toyota.

Tom suddenly jerked the wheel to make an abrupt left turn across a lane of traffic. Brakes squealed. A horn blared. But he made it to the side road and increased his speed. Luckily there wasn't much traffic at ten in the morning on New Year's Day. He glanced into the rearview mirror.

No good. The black minivan was still behind him. And it was gaining.

Unfortunately, the side street wasn't maintained quite as well as the main road. He maneuvered the Toyota deftly over a patch of ice. The smaller size of his vehicle gave him a speed advantage over the minivan. But the Toyota was too light for good traction on slippery blacktop. He skidded around another bend and followed it up with an immediate right turn.

"There, Special Agents Williamson and Marks. Let's see you follow that!" he said.

Again he peered into the rearview mirror. This time, there was no sign of the minivan. He had lost them. Tom exhaled slowly as he pulled to a stop at a red light. Now he just had to make his way to the interstate without being seen again and head west, toward Arizona and Elizabeth. Suddenly the black van appeared out of nowhere. It pulled up directly behind him, looming over his subcompact like a mountain. Tom floored the accelerator, and the Toyota shot through the red light—and onto a thick patch of ice.

Jeff watched breathlessly while Tom struggled to control the Toyota spiraling across the intersection. "He's hit the ice," Keisha said unnecessarily. Then the Toyota slammed against a curb and was still.

Jeff and Keisha leaped from the minivan and ran toward the small car, pistols in hand. A spider-web of cracks showed where Tom's forehead had hit the windshield. A dark trickle of blood streamed down the young man's face. Jeff was glad to see that the injury didn't look serious. Still, he cursed himself. Weren't enough innocent people in danger already? Tom wasn't a criminal; he was just scared out of his mind for his girlfriend's safety. *And I've made things worse by forcing the poor kid into a desperate escape attempt.*

Jeff shrugged back his feelings of sympathy while Keisha yanked open the door and checked over Tom's injury. "It's just a scratch," she pronounced. Jeff could see that she'd been worried as well.

Tom looked resigned. He didn't protest as Keisha pulled him from the car. And he stood still while Jeff slipped a handcuff to Tom's wrist, fastening the other around his own. Innocent or not, Jeff reminded himself, Tom was someone he would have to keep an eye on. He was the only person around who might be able to find the Wakefield twins. Jeff couldn't afford to let Tom escape again.

The trees aren't as thick now, Jessica noticed as the convertible sped through the frozen forest. They'd been traveling downhill for some time and the road was clearer, with only a few patches of ice here and there. But one thing hadn't changed. The barrel of Scott's revolver still burned cold against Jessica's temple.

A sign announced that they would be leaving the Kaibab National Forest in one mile. *What the heck is that?* Jessica asked herself. Kaibab sounded like something to eat. She cursed herself silently. *Why am I such a moron when it comes to geography?* A little knowledge of their location could go a long way toward finding a way to free themselves.

"This is the Kaibab National Forest," Elizabeth said, obviously thinking along the same lines. "That means we're close to the Grand Canyon, right?"

"Give that twin a cigar," Scott said.

"I suppose that's where you plan to dispose of us when you're finished."

"They don't call you the smart twin for nothing, do they?" Scott answered in a smug tone. "Actually, I had a specific place in mind. It's called Marble Plateau, and it's a real pretty place on the northeast part of the Grand Canyon. You'll like it there—easy access, not so many of those eastern tourists around." He began reeling off information about the depth of the canyon and the time it would take to fall to the bottom.

Suddenly Jessica couldn't stand it any longer. *Now's your chance,* a voice whispered in her brain. *Do something now, while Elizabeth has Scott distracted.*

Without thinking, Jessica grabbed Scott's gun with both hands. He struggled against her. The windshield shattered like ice, and a loud report crashed in Jessica's ears. Elizabeth screamed. The car swerved on a patch of snow, and she clutched at the wheel, trying to regain control.

Jessica couldn't breathe. She still fought with Scott for control of the revolver, but he had one powerful arm locked around her neck, cutting off her air. The baseball cap sailed off her head and was gone, floating behind the car like a kite until it disappeared against the blue and white of the mid-morning sky.

"Let go of the gun or you'll choke to death," Scott growled.

Jessica struggled desperately, but she knew she couldn't win. Her grip on the gun barrel was slipping. Scott would wrest the weapon from her. Then he'd drive to his favorite deserted plateau and shoot them both, before dropping their bodies into the Grand Canyon. Her mind was fuzzy from lack of oxygen. She realized she would pass out soon. She would almost welcome the darkness.

A burst of cold air revived her. Elizabeth had let go of the steering wheel and was fighting with Scott to free Jessica and grab the gun. Jessica punched Scott in the face. He swore and grabbed at her hair. The car swerved on another patch of ice, and Scott fell backward. Elizabeth's hand was still on the gun, but Scott had the tighter grip. He swung out with his arm and slammed the barrel into the side of Elizabeth's face. Jessica screamed. She leaned across her reeling sister and reached for the steering wheel as the car spun off the road. But she was too late. The car pitched to one side. Then it flipped into the air, and everything went black.

Scott sat up slowly, rubbing his eyes against the snow's glare. It was damn cold, lying in a field in his jeans and jean jacket. Torn. *How did my jacket get ripped?* he wondered, dazed. He took inventory of himself. Something cold and wet ran down his arm. A rivulet of blood stained the snow, oozing from a cut near his elbow. And his ankle throbbed. His headache was about par for the course, for New Year's Day, he thought wryly. He was sure he hadn't been up drinking all night. Though he wasn't sure exactly what he *had* been doing.

Scott glanced at his watch. It was stopped at ten forty; judging from the shadows in the snow, it wasn't much past that. So he hadn't been unconscious long. And it seemed odd, but there was his Colt .45, glittering in the snow a few feet away. *Now what is that doing on the ground?*

Suddenly the morning's events flooded back over him. Scott sat bolt upright. *The Wakefield twins.* The green T-bird was on the side of the road, a few hundred feet away, dented but upright. "I'm lucky I was thrown when it flipped over," he said aloud. "Nobody could have lived through that."

But it wouldn't hurt to make sure, he decided as his head cleared. He'd been too careless in the last few days; that's why he was in this mess in the first place.

Scott reloaded his revolver and spun the cylinder. Then he stood up and staggered toward the convertible, ready to shoot at any sign of movement.

It was morning. Jessica was lying in her toasty, comfortable bed in the Wakefields' home in Sweet Valley, smelling French toast cooking downstairs. The reddish light that filtered through her eyelids was the warm California sunshine streaming through her window. Any minute now, Prince Albert would come bounding into her pleasantly messy room and lick her face.

Something cold and wet touched Jessica's cheek, and she opened her eyes expectantly. The illusion shattered. She was lying across the front seat of a wrecked T-bird convertible, only her safety belt holding her in place. Her head hung over the side, where she could see a very un-California-like layer of ice on the hard, frozen ground at the side of the road. It was snowing. Big, wet flakes fluttered down on her, gently touching her cheek and coating everything in the crumpled convertible with a frosty, slushy blanket.

"Elizabeth!" she called. Elizabeth slumped in the driver's seat, an ugly, bloody wound in her forehead. Blood was matted in her blond hair and on her wool ski cap. Surprisingly, her dark sunglasses still clung to the bridge of her nose, but now they hung lopsided.

For one confused moment, Jessica thought she was back in a dream. As hard as she tried, she couldn't reach her injured sister. Something kept pulling her back. Then she realized that she was still wearing her seat belt. She struggled to unhitch it.

"Elizabeth!" she cried frantically, bending over her sister. A cold wind made it hard to tell if Elizabeth was breathing. "Lizzie, talk to me, please!"

Then Jessica caught a movement in the cracked side-view mirror. "No," she murmured, shaking her head. "It can't be."

Scott was staggering across a snow-covered field toward the car. Blood dripped from his left arm, but his eyes were determined. And his Colt .45 was pointing directly at her.

Near hysteria, Jessica unbuckled her sister's lifeless body from her seat belt and dumped her into the backseat. "Please be alive, Elizabeth!" she pleaded. Then she grabbed the steering wheel and tried to start the car. "Start, start, start!" she begged, her voice rising on each repetition. Scott was standing ten feet behind the right fender of the convertible.

"This is it, Jessica," he said, raising the gun. "You can't get away."

"Please, ohplease, ohplease!" Jessica screamed at the engine, cold tears spilling from her eyes.

Scott reached the back fin of the T-bird just as the engine roared to life. Jessica gunned the accelerator, cringing as gunshots whizzed by her head. She turned just in time to see Scott leap onto the back of the convertible as it jumped forward.

Chapter
Twelve

Tom walked between Jeff and Keisha, struggling against their hands on his arms. "I don't need your help!" he said, scowling as the three entered the hotel. "Unless you want to help me rescue the twins."

Jeff looked at him sharply. "I thought you didn't know where they are."

"I don't," Tom said with a sidelong glance at Jeff. "But I may have some ideas about how to figure out where they are."

"Then the best way you can help them is to talk to us," Keisha urged, not unkindly. "Believe me, we want to get to the bottom of this as much as you do."

"Then go with me to find them," Tom pleaded. "It's the only way I'm telling you anything, I swear. There's no way I'm letting you people loose on them with Neanderthals like that—"

He pointed to the hulking Agent Brute, who was stalking toward them across the hotel lobby. The brutish man eyed him hungrily, as if Tom were a steak he was about to eat for dinner.

"We're ready for the interrogation," Agent Brute reported. "Should we take him down to the tech room?" He spoke to Jeff, but his eyes never left Tom.

Jeff shook his head. "No, I've changed my mind."

Even Keisha looked surprised.

"I've decided to take him back up to his own room," Jeff explained. "Tom seems to be having trouble with his memory. Maybe something up there will spark it."

"You'd better let us come along," Agent Brute remarked with another menacing glance at Tom. "You might need our . . . special expertise."

Tom met his stare, pretending he wasn't terrified out of his wits. "Expertise at what?" he shot back. "Let me guess. As an encore, you eat puppies."

"That's right," Jeff interjected. "He especially loves 'em with hollandaise. Now cut the chatter, everyone. Are you coming with me, Tom, or what?"

"Do I have a choice?" Tom held up his wrist, which was still handcuffed to Jeff's. The agent had thrown a raincoat over the cuffs so as not to attract attention as they walked through the hotel.

But the steel bit hard and cold into Tom's wrist, a constant reminder that he was stuck in a safe hotel in Vail, while his girlfriend was far away and in trouble.

Keisha hit the up button on the elevator. "Do you want me along, Jeff? Standard operating procedure calls for—"

"Don't lecture me on procedure," Jeff ordered. "I know what I'm doing." He sounded confident, but Tom could've sworn he heard the agent mutter two more words under his breath: "I hope."

As the bell rang for the elevator, Jeff leaned over to whisper something to Keisha. Tom saw her eyes widen. She nodded. Then Jeff dragged Tom into the elevator.

"He's all yours," said Agent Brute as the doors closed. "But call me if you need me."

Jeff punched a button.

"Hey!" Tom yelped. "My room's on the ninth floor. Why are we going all the way to the roof?"

"Change of plans," Jeff said. The big man spoke softly, but his stormy glare silenced Tom.

They stepped out onto the roof of the hotel, and Tom was hit by a blast of cold air. A helicopter was hovering overhead, whipping the winds around them into a frenzy of noise and movement as it descended to a nearby helipad.

"Come on," Jeff ordered, pushing him toward the helicopter.

Tom blinked back tears. Now he understood. The agents' threats about obstruction of justice hadn't been idle ones. Jeff was taking him directly to jail. He'd never find Elizabeth now.

Snow was falling hard and thick. With most of the windshield gone, Jessica could hardly see ahead of her as she slammed her foot on the gas pedal. She jerked the steering wheel. The T-bird obediently swerved across the dotted white line in the center of the road. But Scott hung on. He lay on the back of the car, his legs spread-eagled over the trunk. One strong arm was flung over the seat back, which he gripped tightly despite the deep cut Jessica could see on his elbow. He was dangerously close to Elizabeth's motionless form as she sprawled on the backseat. Scott's other hand still held the gun. He maneuvered himself into position to shoot.

"Dammit, Jess! Stop the car or I'll kill you right here! You can't get away from me!"

Up ahead, Jessica noticed an old barn a few feet from the road, its roof sagging with the weight of wet snow. She spun the steering wheel again, aiming the convertible as if it were a pistol. The car bounced off the road. Then Jessica flung the side of the vehicle against the barn wall, praying that Scott would fall off—and the battered car would hold together.

The car shuddered at the impact, and a sickening scraping sound reminded Jessica of fingernails on a blackboard. Then she was bounding back to the road, and Scott was rolling in the snow near the old barn.

Jessica realized that she was crying. The cold tears ran back along her temples and disappeared into the snowflakes that still streamed by on the unshielded wind. Jessica scrunched down low in the seat to protect her eyes from the gusts. She didn't know whether to feel relieved or terrified. She had finally ditched Scott for good. But Elizabeth hadn't moved an inch.

"Please be alive, Elizabeth," she implored, gazing back at her sister. But she didn't intend to stop the car to learn more about Elizabeth's condition.

Suddenly she realized that the snowstorm had stopped abruptly at the edge of the forest. Now the car sped through a tiny settlement. "House something-or-other," she read aloud, catching what she could of the sign as she sped past. The town sat on one end of a wide, treeless plateau where thin patches of snow veiled amber outcroppings of rock. She thought about stopping for help. But she didn't dare. First she would put a few miles between herself and Scott.

Scott was gone, but Jessica imagined his cold gray eyes, mocking her. And she heard his deep, throaty voice above the whistling of the wind through her shattered windshield. "You can't get away from me!" he had said. She prayed that he had been wrong.

The helicopter's clatter made it hard for Tom to think. He had failed. He had been caught, without reaching Elizabeth and her sister. Now they would probably die. They would be shot dead by an overeager cop, an FBI thug like that brute in the hotel, or the killer who was really responsible for robbing the store in Nevada. For all he knew, the twins could be dead already. And all he would have to show for his efforts would be a prison term for obstructing justice.

He stared out the open doorway of the helicopter, half blinded by tears of frustration. The hotel receded beneath him. Around it, tiny skiers dotted the slopes, carefree, their round little late-morning shadows visible beneath them. They swarmed over the slopes as if it were a normal New Year's Day—as if hope were still alive. As the helicopter rose, they merged into the winter landscape and vanished.

Jeff unlocked the handcuffs. For a moment, Tom thought he was going to push him from the helicopter. Then Jeff turned to him with a grim smile.

"Okay, partner," Jeff said. "Now that we've ditched Agent Brute and the rest, tell the pilot where we're going so she can bring us to your friends. Let's find those fugitive twins of yours before they get themselves hurt."

* * *

"You're going to be okay," Jessica told Elizabeth over her shoulder. The convertible whipped eastward across the wide plateau. Elizabeth lay unmoving in the backseat. "Just hang on, Liz. Please hang on."

Jessica didn't know how long Elizabeth had been unconscious, but it seemed like an hour. Jessica guessed that it was about noon. The lengthy shadows of morning had dwindled into spots of blue shade in the snow.

"Where are we?" murmured a soft voice behind her. For a moment, Jessica thought she'd imagined it in the whistling of the wind. Then she almost fainted from relief. Elizabeth still looked weak, but at last her eyes were open.

"Oh, Liz," Jessica breathed, "you can't believe how happy I am to see you awake! I was so worried about you."

"What happened?"

"We hit a patch of ice, and the car flipped completely over." She bit her lip. "I thought you were dead."

"Where's Scott?" Elizabeth asked, struggling to sit up.

"Don't try to get up! You need to rest," Jessica ordered. "I guess Scott wasn't wearing a seat belt. He was thrown out of the car when we went over."

"Is he dead?"

"Unfortunately not. He came after us, and he started shooting at me."

"My God, Jessica!"

"I finally got the car going. Scott jumped on the back as I pulled away, and I had to ram the car into the side of a barn to knock him off. It was about fifteen minutes ago, just before a little town we went through."

"What town?" Elizabeth asked. "Do you have any idea where we are?"

Jessica shrugged. "The name of the town had 'House' in it, but I didn't catch the rest."

"That sounds familiar. I must have seen something like it on the map. What about Scott? Was he hurt?"

"He was limping a little, and his arm was bleeding from the accident." She smiled darkly. "Unfortunately, it wasn't his gun arm."

"I mean, after you knocked him off the car."

"Maybe, but not too badly. I watched him roll in the snow when he fell, and then I saw him sit up as we drove away."

"Jessica, we have to go back for him!"

"I think you'd better lie down, Liz. You must have a more serious head injury than I thought."

"My head injury isn't serious, but I am. Turn the car around."

"Elizabeth, he tried to shoot me!"

"I know. But what were you planning to do on our own? It's only a matter of time before the police catch up with us again. And they still think we're armed and dangerous."

"So we'll show them we're not. We'll tell them about Scott. I don't know! We'll *make* them believe us."

"They're likely to shoot us first, Jessica, and then find out we don't have an arsenal in our backpacks."

"And I suppose you have a better idea."

"Not yet. We have to come up with a plan— some way to find Scott and stop him before the police show up. Then we can turn him over to them, and they'll see that he's been the dangerous one all along."

"You're out of your mind! He's a homicidal maniac, Liz. We finally got away from him, and you want to turn around and go back looking for him?"

"Jessica, you said there was a town back there. Let's drive back to the town and just scout it out."

"What good will that do?"

"We haven't heard the news since early this morning. For all we know, the FBI might have figured out Scott's the killer by now. Maybe the police are after him instead of us. How can we make a decision about what to do next unless we have all the facts?"

"Okay, then let's get all the facts, right now." Jessica flicked on the radio and began hunting for a station. "At least it still works."

Music poured out of the radio.

"Maybe not that station," Elizabeth said.

Jessica turned the dial again. There were several music stations, but no news. She turned it off.

"Okay, so the radio wasn't a good idea. But neither is going back toward Scott. I'd rather face the FBI than Scott Culver any day. I don't think you understand, Liz. He shot at me!"

"So did the police," Elizabeth reminded her.

"I'm afraid of him!" Jessica protested, remembering the cruel glint in his steel-gray eyes.

"I'm afraid of him, too," Elizabeth admitted quietly. "Isn't that all the more reason to want him where we can keep an eye on him? Remember what happened last time we thought we were free of him. He showed up in the backseat of our car and tried to kill us again."

"That isn't going to happen this time. He's miles behind us."

"Jessica, he knows this terrain better than he knows his own face. If he can get hold of a car in that town we passed, how do you know he won't take some shortcut and cut us off somewhere ahead?"

"And how do you know that he will?"

"If we have to face him down someplace, I'd rather do it in the middle of a town, with people around. If someone else sees him threatening us, maybe people will realize that he's the dangerous one, not us. It's the only way we'll ever prove that we're innocent."

Jessica sighed. As usual, Elizabeth had her at a disadvantage. She was so good at sounding reasonable that she could manage it even when she was talking nonsense.

"Oh, God!" Elizabeth's eyes were wide.

"What is it?" Jessica asked over her shoulder. "Are you all right back there?"

"Jess, did you ever look inside that canvas duffel bag Scott carried around everywhere?"

Jessica snorted. "Look? He wouldn't even let me touch it. Back in Vegas, I think he even showered with the filthy thing. It never left his side."

"It's left his side now," Elizabeth said. "It was shoved way under the seat. It didn't even fall out when the car turned over. It's here, Jess. And it's full of guns."

"But he had his revolver with him."

Elizabeth nodded. "He had one revolver with him," she said, riffling through the bag. "And he has one revolver in this bag, along with a semiautomatic something-or-other." Then she held up a grayish pistol, so small that it looked like a toy. "And I think they call this little one a Saturday night special."

"Get rid of them, quick!"

"Are you crazy? Why would we want to do that?"

"Am *I* crazy? Elizabeth, this means the police are right. We are armed and dangerous!"

"Yes, I suppose we are," Elizabeth said in a low voice.

"What happens if they catch us with all those guns in the car—the car that's probably been reported stolen, since I told Rick we only needed to borrow it for twenty minutes? We'll be shipped off to Alcatraz before we have a chance to open our mouths."

"They don't use Alcatraz as a prison anymore."

"Okay, so we'll be shipped off to San Quentin or something—what do I look like, a travel agent? What the heck does it matter which prison? Just throw the stupid guns out of the car, Liz."

"You're the one who says you're so scared of Scott! Jessica, with these guns, we'll have a fighting chance against him, if it comes to that."

"Elizabeth, we don't even know how to use those guns!"

"So we'll figure it out. Besides, what if we do throw them out of the car and Scott's following us? We'll be handing him more weapons to kill us with! Jessica, don't you see? The only way out of this is to go back and find him—before the police find us!"

Jessica bit her lip. Then she nodded slightly, and began to swing the T-bird around in a wide U-turn. As she did, she noticed something up ahead. "It looks as if we would have to turn back anyhow," she said. "There's a roadblock up ahead."

Elizabeth leaned forward. "Where? Is it the police?"

"No, just a little guardhouse with a wooden gate across the road," Jessica said as she steered the car back toward the west. "The sign said something about this part of Grand Canyon National Park being closed for the winter."

Elizabeth nodded. "So that's where we are. I've heard that some of the roads around the canyon are closed all winter long. It usually snows a lot this time of year."

"It doesn't seem like enough snow to close a road for."

"Well, it's been a warm December. We're lucky it's not as deep as usual, or we'd never have made it this far."

"Does that mean the Grand Canyon is back there? I didn't see it."

"It must be a few miles farther," Elizabeth said with a shrug. "I think this is that Marble Plateau place that Scott mentioned."

Jessica glanced around at the snow-dusted expanse of mauve and reddish-gold rock. From far away, the plateau had looked almost flat. But now that she was in the middle of it, Jessica saw a landscape strewn with low, irregularly shaped peaks and rounded hills, each one outlined in powdery snow.

"It doesn't look like marble," she murmured, thinking of the slick, elegant pillars at Caesars Palace. That was real marble—beautiful, civilized, and totally safe. Not like this strange, forbidding land that looked devoid of life yet seemed to hide the threat of an unspeakable malice. *Was it really only two days ago that we drove through Las Vegas, three college students on an innocent road trip?*

But remembering Caesars Palace made Jessica think of Scott's passionate kiss in the gazebo by the glowing swimming pool. *How could I have been so wrong about him?* she asked herself tearfully.

"How far is that town?" Elizabeth asked.

"I don't know. A few miles, I guess."

Elizabeth's face was grim. "Do you think Scott will be there?"

"How the heck should I know? I know we need to find him. But I hope we don't. I never want to see him again as long as I live." Jessica shuddered, thinking about what she had just said.

She had a feeling that once she saw Scott, she wouldn't live very long at all.

Jeff leaned close to Tom's ear, to be heard over the roar of the helicopter. "So what do you say?" he asked. "Are you going to trust me now and tell me everything you know about Elizabeth's trip, and about her current location?"

Tom glared at him. "Why should I trust you?"

"Because I want to help your girlfriend and her sister."

"I thought you wanted to arrest them for murder and armed robbery."

"I did. But I think I know them better now. And I've become convinced that they're not criminals."

Tom shook his head. "You're only saying that to get me to help you."

Jeff sighed. He needed Tom to trust him. "I had the surveillance video analyzed," he explained. "We couldn't see it at first, but there's a man standing behind Jessica's hat. My theory is that he's the real murderer."

Tom's eyes widened. "Is he still with them?"

"I don't know. But if he is, Jessica and Elizabeth could be in a lot of danger. I believe you know where they are, Tom. Are you going to tell me?"

Tom stared into his eyes for a full minute, as if sizing him up. "Sangwav, Arizona," he said finally. "That's the name of the town Elizabeth called me from today."

"What else did she say?"

"She didn't really *say* anything," Tom said. "She barely had time to tell me it was her. Then she kind of gasped; it was almost like a scream. Then she was gone."

"So how do you know the name of the town she was in?" Jeff asked, confused.

Tom looked embarrassed. "I, um, had the call traced."

Jeff's eyebrows shot up. "Would you mind telling me how a college student manages to get a call traced?"

Tom shrugged. "You must have a complete dossier on me by now. If you do, you know I work for the campus television station at school. As a reporter, I—uh, have my sources."

Jeff had to hand it to the kid. He certainly was resourceful. "Don't worry, I won't ask who your sources are. At least, not right now."

"Do you know where Sangwav is?" Tom asked. "I've never heard of it."

"I don't know where it is. But I do know that *sangwav* is the Paiute word for sin."

"Now, that's a comforting thought."

"Don't worry, kid. I'll put in a call to Keisha. She can track down the town for us in an instant."

"There's something else you should know," Tom said abruptly. "Jessica and Elizabeth weren't driving alone on their trip."

"What?"

"Elizabeth called me the day she left home. She said they'd picked up a hitchhiker near the California-Nevada border. She said he was on his way to Vail and his car broke down."

Jeff narrowed his eyes. This was sounding worse and worse. "That sounds suspicious," he said. "It's too convenient that they should pass a stranded motorist who just happened to be going to the same place they were. Elizabeth doesn't seem like the type to be so thoughtless."

"She's not," Tom said. "But she's got a soft spot for her sister. Apparently Jessica thought he

242

was good looking. And Jess is a master at manipulating her sister into doing whatever she wants her to do."

"I wouldn't really call Jessica manipulative," Jeff began, forgetting that he'd never actually met either twin. Then he let the subject drop. This was no time for defending Jessica's honor. Right now, he was more interested in her life. "Did Elizabeth tell you the hitchhiker's name?"

Tom shrugged. "She did, but I can't remember it. Scott something."

In his mind, Jeff saw the man with the light-brown hair, rising up from the shadows behind Jessica's Stetson hat. He grasped Tom by the shoulders. "Think, Tom! It's important. Scott what?"

Tom buried his face in his hands. "I don't know. I just don't know."

"House Rock, Arizona." Scott read the sign aloud. "Not much of a town, but it'll do just fine."

He stopped at the west end of Main Street to check himself over. His arm had stopped bleeding, and his ankle didn't seem to be broken. He tucked his shirt into his jeans and tried to brush the dirt off his jacket. He smoothed down his thick, light-brown hair and took a deep breath.

A little scruffy around the edges, he thought. *But I bet a lot of people are after New Year's Eve. I shouldn't attract much notice.*

243

He just wished he had his duffel bag. He was glad he'd had the Colt with him when he was thrown from the car. He had some spare ammo in his jacket pockets. But the rest was in the duffel bag, with his other weapons.

The bag must have fallen out of the convertible when Elizabeth flipped it over, he figured. But what if it hadn't? Either the twins had found his pawnshop guns and were hoping to use them for self-defense—or, more likely, the weapons were still tucked away safely in the bag, pushed under the seat where they wouldn't notice it. If that was true, the cops would have a field day if they ever caught up to the girls.

But the cops aren't going to catch up to them, he reminded himself. *Not until I take care of them. A whole arsenal won't be much good to two little college girls who couldn't shoot a fly with a rubber band.* He grinned, but his eyes remained dead cold.

Scott sauntered into a nearby saloon. Sure enough, the patrons were paying more attention to the Rose Bowl game on television than to one tattered stranger. He slipped into the men's room to clean himself up. Then he sat at the bar and ordered a beer and lunch.

Scott was in no hurry. He knew Jessica and Elizabeth. He knew how their minds worked. As clearly as if he'd been sitting beside Elizabeth in the backseat of the T-bird, he saw them driving toward the canyon. Then he saw them turning back. After all, the road was closed for the winter. More important, the drive east would have allowed the girls just enough time to weigh their options and realize that finding Scott was their best bet for clearing their names. He was sure they were heading back in this direction—it was only a matter of time. He patted the revolver through his jacket and leaned back in his chair. When the twins arrived, Scott Culver would be waiting for them. And this time, they wouldn't escape.

Chapter
Thirteen

Elizabeth poked at her sunglasses. The plastic frames had been bent in the accident, and they no longer remained straight across the bridge of her nose. She gave up in disgust. Elizabeth had never been as concerned as her sister about always looking good. But now she felt positively disgusting. She hadn't showered since Las Vegas. Her clothes and hair were covered with the reddish dust of the Nevada desert, the wet snows of the high plateau, her own blood, and a lot of nervous sweat.

"It's bad enough being an identical twin when you're a fugitive from the law," Elizabeth said as they approached the small settlement at the edge of the national forest. "But it's really the pits being an identical twin with a bloody head wound. How am I going to stay inconspicuous while we try to find Scott?"

Jessica's face twisted into a frown. "I hadn't

thought of that. Well, here's that town. Let's stop on a side street where nobody can see us. Then we'll see if we can clean you up."

The damaged car wheezed in protest as she steered it onto a slushy path and parked it behind an abandoned shed.

Elizabeth climbed out of the car and looked around. "I don't know about this place, Jess. From the car, we can't see the main road or the town at all. If Scott or the police come, we won't even know it until they stick their heads—and their guns—around the side."

Jessica shrugged, still sitting in the car. "Look at it this way. If we can't see the police, then the police can't see us either."

Elizabeth noticed that Jessica avoided mentioning the possibility of Scott creeping up on them, unseen. *He really has her spooked,* she thought, concerned and more than a little curious. Something had happened between Jessica and Scott that night in Las Vegas. Elizabeth was sure of it. But Jessica, with a mouth the size of the Grand Canyon, had kept unusually quiet about it. *Obviously Jessica thought she had Scott wrapped around her finger. And she's furious at him for turning against her.* Elizabeth shuddered at the idea of any woman being attracted to a vicious, duplicitous snake like Scott, even if he was good looking. But good taste in men had never been Jessica's strong point.

Elizabeth silently thanked fate for bringing her together with smart, caring, sexy Tom. She wondered what he was doing at that moment, in Vail. And she couldn't help wondering if she would ever see him again.

"Anyway, we don't have much choice," Jessica said. "We've got to make ourselves as invisible as we can before anyone sees us. We'll only be here for a couple minutes. Let me look at that cut on your forehead."

"I wish we had something to clean it with," Elizabeth replied, feeling dirtier than ever.

"Yeah. It's too bad Rick the store clerk had only a '66 T-bird. I should have flirted with a guy who owned a stretch limo, complete with a wet bar and hot tub!"

Elizabeth laughed and clambered into the front seat, over a right-side door that no longer opened. *Leave it to Jessica to make jokes at a time like this.* Despite her twin's knack for getting into trouble, Elizabeth knew there was no one she'd rather be running for her life with.

"Didn't we have some of that mineral water left? We could use that to clean up with."

Jessica searched along the floor of the car. "I don't see any. The bottles must have fallen out when the car flipped over."

"Then I'll just have to cover the blood with my ski cap."

"That's no good," Jessica pointed out. "The

cap has blood on it too. I know. If we roll up the edge a little higher, we can cover the stained part." She replaced the wool cap on Elizabeth's head.

"How does it look?" Elizabeth asked.

"Not great, but it'll do, if people don't stare at us too closely. Put your hair up underneath it—it's better if nobody sees that we're blond." Suddenly she froze. "Oh, God, Liz. Is that a siren?"

Elizabeth strained to hear. "It sounds like it's far away—maybe it has nothing to do with us."

"Probably not," Jessica said lightly, but she didn't look convinced.

Both twins held their breath as the siren's call grew louder. Then it stopped. They exhaled together.

"False alarm," Elizabeth said gratefully. "I guess we can get back to camouflaging ourselves."

Jessica peered into the cracked side-view mirror. "You know, I never thought of being blond, beautiful, and the center of attention as a problem before."

Elizabeth raised her eyebrows. "Obviously, excessive modesty isn't either."

"You know what I mean! Inconspicuous just isn't something I have much practice with." She frowned at her reflection. "But to tell you the truth, my hair's so filthy it's hard to tell what color it is."

"Well, you have to disguise yourself somehow. People here have probably seen that video on TV, too. At least cover your hair."

"My baseball cap's gone. It blew away when I was fighting with Scott for the gun." She pawed through the glove compartment for the patterned silk scarf she'd been wearing earlier. "It's pretty wrinkled, but it will have to do."

Elizabeth rolled her eyes at the thought of a fugitive Jessica, running for her life but still worried about a wrinkled scarf. Suddenly she gripped her sister's arm. "Shhhh!"

"What is it?"

"I don't know. A motor." The whining sound increased steadily in volume. "A car, I guess, heading this way. Maybe it's the police."

"I don't hear any sirens."

"Me neither. Quiet! It's really close."

Jessica smiled and shook her head. "It's okay. I recognize that sound. It's only a motorcycle, driving out of town toward the canyon. It has nothing to do with us. I'm sure the police and the FBI have a much bigger welcome wagon in store for the armed and dangerous Wakefield Gang."

"Just the same, let's stay hidden here until it's gone. We shouldn't take chances on anyone seeing us and the car together. If Rick filed a stolen-car report, the FBI will know it's us driving this thing."

"What was that call?" Tom yelled over the noise of the helicopter. "Any word on the twins?" He prayed that the news was good.

251

Jeff handed the headset back to the pilot. "Keisha just got two reports out of Arizona," he said, his chin close to Tom's ear. "First, she heard something from that town you mentioned—Sangwav. The police there got a call on a car stolen this morning—a '66 Thunderbird convertible, green. It sounds as if it was our girls who took it."

"But Elizabeth and Jessica would never—"

"Both of the young women had their hair covered," Jeff continued, forcefully, until Tom closed his mouth. "One was wearing dark sunglasses, but the other definitely had blue eyes."

"Lots of people have blue eyes—"

"The one with the sunglasses was talking on the telephone," Jeff said. "The other was buying some things at the counter. Then she got hold of the car keys, grabbed her sister, and ran out of there."

Tom gasped. "That could have been Elizabeth's call to me!"

"I think so. My guess is that Jessica sweet-talked a store clerk out of the convertible, saying she needed to borrow it for a few minutes. After four hours, the cashier finally reported it stolen."

Tom opened his mouth to protest, but Jeff held up a hand. "I know what you're going to say. Jessica would never steal a car. I agree that she normally wouldn't. But maybe she was desperate. Or maybe she really did plan to borrow it for only a little while. Either way, I've got every law-enforcement officer in northern Arizona watching for that T-bird—with orders not to shoot unless absolutely necessary."

"Will they follow the orders?"

Jeff stared at him gravely, and Tom knew the answer. In two days' time, the pretty, golden-haired Wakefield twins had become a local legend—beautiful but deadly. Tom sighed. There might as well have been a bounty on Elizabeth and Jessica's blond heads.

"The other report just came in from the U.S. Park Police in Kaibab National Forest," Jeff continued. "There was some sort of accident on the edge of the forest, not far from a town called House Rock. Keisha already sent the local sheriff's office there to work with the park police. From the tracks in the snow and from the skid marks on the road, it seems that a vehicle about the size of a T-bird slid on the ice and actually flipped over."

Tom closed his eyes. "Oh, God!" he choked out, imagining Elizabeth's lifeless body sprawled across the frozen ground.

"Hold on, Tom. The car wasn't there when the police arrived, so somebody must have driven it away from the accident."

"How do we know it was them?"

"The stolen convertible had a broken top. I guess practically everything inside the car tumbled out when the vehicle turned over. The police found a lot of debris strewn around the accident site. Among other things, there were articles of women's clothing, size six."

Tom nodded.

"They also found several bottles of mineral water and a box of cookies."

Tom remembered Jessica's latest junk-food habit. "Chocolate chip?"

Jeff looked surprised. "Yes, I think that's what Keisha said. And one officer found a woman's handbag in a nearby ditch. Jessica's driver's license was inside."

Tom took a deep breath, not sure if the news was good or bad. At least it was a solid lead.

Jeff's deep brown eyes filled with concern. "Tom," he said gently, "the police found one other thing at the accident site."

"What?"

"There was blood in the snow. Not a lot of it," he added quickly. "And we don't have an identification yet. Forensics is typing it now."

Tom nodded slowly. "How much longer until we reach this House Rock place?"

"Only a few minutes," Jeff said with a weak smile. "I've instructed the pilot to follow the Colorado River along the Grand Canyon. She says visibility is good today. If there's a green convertible along the rim somewhere, we ought to be able to see it."

"So you think they're still in the area?"

"I can't say for sure. But my guess is that they

are. There really aren't that many other places they could be—most of the roads along the canyon are closed for the winter. And I don't think the twins crossed the Colorado River."

"Why not?"

"There's only one bridge. Our patrols would have spotted them on it. Tom, what about this guy Jessica picked up? Have you been able to remember his last name?"

"Sort of," Tom said. "It was Carver, or something like that. Do you know anything about a Scott Carver?"

"Not offhand. But I'll radio it in to Keisha and see what she can find out."

The twins stepped onto Main Street. Jessica's knees wobbled, but she forced herself to march on cheerfully. "The sign says the town is called House Rock," she said. "What a dorky name. It's almost as bad as Sangwang!"

"Sangwav," Elizabeth corrected.

"It's almost as bad as that, too. So what's this brilliant plan of yours? How are we going to catch Scott? And prove to the FBI that he's the real murderer?"

"I don't know yet."

Jessica felt her chest tightening. "You brought me back here to risk our lives—and you don't even have a plan?"

Elizabeth shrugged. "We've got weapons of

our own now. And we're in a town. There must be some people around. Maybe he'll make a mistake in a public place, with witnesses. Or maybe we can help him slip up. If Scott confesses when there's another person close by, we'll be home free."

Jessica whirled on her sister, incredulous. "Get him to confess? Now why didn't I think of that? God, Liz, it's great to have a genius along."

"I know you're scared," Elizabeth said quietly, "but don't take it out on me."

Jessica stared at her. Elizabeth was infuriating. But as usual, she was right.

It's my fault that we're in this mess, Jessica reminded herself. *I owe it to Liz to be a little more cooperative.* She nodded. "All right," she said in a low voice. "We'll make up the rest of the plan as we go along. But what should we do first?"

"First we have to find out if Scott's been here, and if he's still here. I think we should split up— we're more conspicuous together."

"No way," Jessica said with a shudder. "I'm more afraid of Scott than I am of the police or the FBI. I'm staying with you."

"Fine. Where should we go first?"

Jessica looked around. "There's a store, a bar, and a gas station on this block. I guess we just start asking people about him. But you'd better bring along that duffel bag—just in case."

* * *

Jeff took a set of earphones from the helicopter pilot. He bent his head, as if that would keep the drone of the chopper from interfering with his conversation.

"Jeff?" crackled Keisha's voice over the headset. "I've got an update on the Oldsmobile sedan found on I-15 in California."

"Who's it registered to?" Jeff demanded. "Anyone in our files?"

"Sorry to disappoint you. The Olds is registered to a Frank and Nancy Dixon, an elderly couple with no criminal record whatsoever. They reported it stolen at the end of last August."

Jeff sighed. He stared at Tom, who sat a few feet away. *Poor kid,* he thought. *I hate telling him that another lead hasn't panned out. At least we've got a general idea of where the twins are.*

"Did you turn up anything on a Scott Carver?" he asked Keisha.

"Sorry, I can't find anyone with that name in our files."

"Damn! This Scott guy is the key, I'm sure of it. When we find him, we'll find those girls. See if you can turn up anyone with a similar last name."

"I can try, but I doubt I'll find anything very useful."

"I know—we seem to be hitting dead ends everywhere we turn. My only hope now is that we'll just happen to see a green convertible driving along the rim of the canyon."

"Don't sound so glum, Jeff. At least you've made Frank and Nancy Dixon happy. You never know when you might need a few friends in Bozeman, Montana."

"Bozeman, Montana?"

"The Dixons live in Bozeman. Why? Does that mean something to you?"

"Not exactly, but it might be another connection. There was a series of holdups beginning last fall in Montana and Wyoming. They looked similar to the Utah and Nevada incidents, but the evidence was cold."

"I think we just warmed it up a little."

"I hope so. Keish, check Montana state criminal records, especially around Bozeman, for the time period when that car was stolen."

"What am I looking for?"

"Somebody with the first name Scott and a last name similar to Carver. I have a hunch that this time it's going to pan out."

Scott sped past the rickety old shed that marked the eastern outskirts of House Rock. He breathed deeply of the crisp, cold air, loving the rush of power that always streamed through his body as he commanded the open road from the saddle of a motorcycle.

Scott had borrowed the bike from a gullible, wide-eyed girl at the local service station, right after he'd heard a police siren in the distance.

Maybe the cops came across the accident site in the forest, he speculated. Surely they couldn't have found the twins. Scott was positive that the Wakefields were somewhere east of House Rock— between the town and the Grand Canyon.

Most likely, Scott decided, the police siren had nothing to do with him or the Wakefields. But it wouldn't do to wait around town and find out. He'd sweet-talked a vehicle from the first girl he saw—and it was a Harley-Davidson, no less. Then he'd hightailed it out of House Rock, heading east across Marble Plateau toward the Grand Canyon.

This was the only road that led from town. Jessica and Elizabeth would be on it, too. And they must have heard the siren in the forest. They wouldn't risk capture by the FBI, so they would have fled from that siren, toward the Grand Canyon.

"Besides," he reasoned, "I know these girls won't rest until they've found me. If they made it to House Rock, then they would have snooped around just long enough to learn where I've headed. They'll follow me."

Scott glanced behind him, suddenly alert. Was that another siren? He gripped the motorcycle tighter with his lean, muscular thighs. As he shifted position, he felt the comforting pressure of his Colt .45 against his side. Again the siren seemed to be behind him, in the woods. But he wasn't taking any chances. Luckily he knew this part of the country as well as any local cop. He decided to detour off the road, in case the FBI was on his tail. He'd head cross-country toward the canyon, taking a shortcut he knew, to head off Jessica and Elizabeth when they showed up in the green T-bird. Then he would force them to carry out the final phase of a new plan that was brewing in his mind.

Scott laughed out loud. His plan was perfect. It would keep Jessica and Elizabeth from ratting on him, permanently. And nobody would ever connect him to their deaths. Then he would proceed to Mexico, as free as a bird—thanks to the Wakefields' tragic demise.

He imagined their eulogy. *Two college coeds— the products of an idyllic upbringing—grow bored with their squeaky-clean existence. Thirsting for adventure, they embark on a crime spree that begins as a vacation lark and balloons out of control. The nice-girls-turned-bad elude the cops and the FBI, leading the authorities on a chase through two states. Then, consumed with guilt and panic, the girls launch their T-bird off the snow-lined rim of the Grand Canyon and plummet to the rocky bed of the Colorado River, a mile below.*

Scott gunned the engine and steered the bike onto the flat expanse of rock that stretched away on both sides of the road. The plaintive voices of police sirens dwindled in the distance. He was safe. And soon, he would be free.

"What did she say?" Tom demanded as Jeff handed the headphones back to the pilot. Keisha Williamson had just radioed with another update, and Tom could tell from the look on Jeff's face that there was news. "Did she find a Scott somebody in Montana?"

"Yes, she did," Jeff said gravely. "There's a long file on a Scott Culver who fits the general description."

Tom snapped his fingers. "Culver! I think that's it! What's his story?"

"It isn't pretty. Scott Culver is wanted for violent felonies in five states. Murder, armed robbery—you name it. He's been arrested and tried on lesser charges several times in the past."

"Then why isn't he in prison?"

"He was in a state penitentiary near Bozeman, Montana. He got out last August, after serving two years of a five-year term for—guess what?—armed robbery. Since he's been out, he seems to have become smarter; he's a real pro at covering his tracks. I guess he learned a few tricks from his neighbors in the pen."

"And people say prisoners don't get enough education."

"Scott Culver's had plenty of education—all the wrong kind. The police have no record of his current whereabouts. In fact, he's wanted in Montana for parole violations; the authorities think he left the state almost as soon as he was released from prison."

"How will you find out if he's our man?"

"Keisha has Culver's file on computer. But she hasn't received his photo from Washington yet. So she can't say if he matches the picture in the video."

Tom frowned. Jeff—the imperturbable FBI agent—actually looked frightened.

"I hope to God he's not the guy the twins were traveling with," Jeff continued. "If he is, then Jessica and Elizabeth are in worse trouble than we thought. Scott Culver sounds like bad news. Real bad."

Elizabeth stepped out of the dim saloon and blinked in the stark winter sunlight. Jessica followed a minute later.

"At least we know we're on the right track," Elizabeth said. "The bartender said that someone who looked like Scott was in for a sandwich just a half hour ago."

"That's more than I learned from those animals watching the Rose Bowl," Jessica said with a grimace. "Though if I'd been in the market for dates, I'd be busy every Saturday night until I'm eighty."

Elizabeth wasn't listening to her. "Look at that girl," she said, pointing to the mechanic at the service station across the street. "She looks about our age. I bet she'd have noticed if a guy walked by looking as good as Scott does."

They hurried toward the striking redhead, who was leaning over the hood of an ancient Buick, her mane of tousled curls trailing in grease.

"Women are smarter than men," Jessica reminded Elizabeth in a whisper. "Let's not give her the chance to see that we're twins. You stay back—I'll do the talking."

Elizabeth looked skeptical, but she shrugged.

Jessica smiled her most engaging grin. "Hi! I'm . . . Jennifer!" she said brightly, showing the dimple in her left cheek. Elizabeth faced the display of motor oils and eavesdropped on the conversation.

"I'm Sophie," the redhead replied through a wad of chewing gum.

"Have you seen a really good-looking guy come through town?" Jessica asked in her flightiest voice. "I danced with him last night at a New Year's Eve party in Sang—uh, I mean in Jacob Lake."

Sophie examined a dipstick. "I think I know who you mean. The guy isn't too tall, but he's got a great bod—lots of muscles, but slim. And he has thick, light-brown hair you want to run your fingers through. Is that the one?"

"That sure sounds like him," Jessica said. "Kind of a cowboy type."

The mechanic tossed her curly hair. "Yeah,

well, if you wanted a date for tonight, I'm afraid you're out of luck." She popped her chewing gum. "Sam—that's his name—came out of the bar across the street twenty minutes ago and practically begged me to go out with him tonight."

Elizabeth noticed that Jessica hesitated a moment before speaking. *Jessica's jealous!* Elizabeth realized, surprised. *After everything he's put us through, she's still attracted to Scott!* Suddenly Elizabeth understood just how difficult this day had been for Jessica. *She must hate herself for still feeling that way about him.*

"Oh, that's not it at all," Jessica told Sophie. "Sam and I, um, we have some business to discuss. I was supposed to have lunch with him, but I was late getting here. And now I'd really like to catch up with, uh, Sam."

Sophie shrugged. "Shouldn't be too hard. The road east is a straight shot from here to the canyon. No turnoffs, no nothing. You're bound to catch him either coming or going—he rode out that way less than fifteen minutes ago."

Jessica began to turn away, but stopped. "Rode on what?" she asked. "I, uh, thought his car broke down."

The redhead nodded sympathetically. "It did. I told him to have it towed here and I'd fix it up for him, for free. In the meantime, he wanted to drive out to the Grand Canyon, so I insisted that he borrow my Harley."

"So he's on a motorcycle?"

"Yup. He'll be bringing it back tonight, in time for our date."

"You said he rode east from here?" Jessica asked sharply. Elizabeth knew she was thinking of the bike they'd heard leaving town a little while before.

Come on, Jessica, she urged silently. *We've got the information we needed. Now let's get out of here!*

"Uh-oh!" Sophie exclaimed, noting Jessica's urgent expression. "I've probably told you something I shouldn't have. Sam owes you money, doesn't he? Now he'll be mad at me for telling you where he went. And—"

"It's all right, Sophie!" Jessica interrupted. "He doesn't owe me money. In fact, I'm the one who owes *him* something. And I'm going to make sure that cowboy gets exactly what he deserves."

Chapter Fourteen

The snow-covered plateau looked flat from a distance. But now that he was in the middle of it, Scott could see the familiar undulations of sandy mounds and water-carved ridges. Overland riding wasn't easy; the terrain grew bumpier as he neared the canyon. Scott slowed the motorcycle, remembering that the twins were driving a clunky old T-bird. Surely they had noticed the dark track in the snow where his Harley had left the road. They must be on his trail by now. All he had to do was allow them enough time to catch up with him. Then he would head straight for the Grand Canyon.

He glanced into his rearview mirror and relaxed. "And here they come," he said into the wind. A green convertible had appeared behind him and was quickly closing the distance between itself and his bike. Elizabeth was at the wheel.

Scott steered the bike into a gully that might have been a dry creek bed. The ground was smoother here; it would be easier for the twins to follow him. The Grand Canyon was only a half-mile away, he knew. But it was invisible behind a row of cliffs that rose up in front of the motorcycle, their layers of gray, red, and amber rock glowing through a dusting of white snow.

Scott smiled a self-satisfied grin. Jessica and Elizabeth were unfamiliar with the terrain, and they had no map. The twins would never know how close they were to the gorge until it was too late. And then he would force them and their borrowed T-bird over the edge, into the gaping, sheer-sided canyon.

Suddenly Scott discerned a new note in the steady hum of the Harley. For an instant, he considered pulling over to check the motorcycle's engine. But it soon became clear that the *thwonk-thwonk-thwonk* was not emanating from the bike. And it was getting louder.

Normally, Tom would have been fascinated by the view of the Grand Canyon from the helicopter. Rock strata lined the sheer sides of the majestic canyon in shades of mauve and gold and terra-cotta, all laced with pure white snow. Beautiful, eerie formations rose like temples from its depths. And a mile below the Colorado River dashed along, a glistening ribbon in the afternoon sun.

But now, Tom's sense of urgency outweighed his awe. Elizabeth was down there somewhere. And Scott Culver, a crazed killer, was either with her or after her. Keisha had called Jeff again a moment before. The forensics report from the accident site was in, and the match on the blood was positive. Scott had been there at Kaibab National Forest when the convertible the twins borrowed had flipped over in the snow.

"I have a hunch we won't find them near this part of the canyon," Jeff said. "There's an area northeast of here called Marble Plateau. It's closer to their last known position. It's part of the Grand Canyon, but it's very steep, and it's a lot narrower than most of this you see below us. And the ground's pretty flat for quite a ways around. If they are there, we should be able to spot them right away."

"Mary," he called to the pilot, "head north along the river, toward Lees Ferry. That's where we'll locate our fugitives."

Tom took a deep breath. He was glad to have Jeff working with him. In some ways, the FBI agent was a mystery. The man's eyes were filled with pain, as if he could never be at peace. Tom had seen enough of Jeff to know that he could be gruff, even rude at times. But whatever else he might have on his mind, Jeff seemed to care about the twins. In fact, he had an almost religious fervor about bringing them home safely—especially Jessica, for some reason.

The canyon rushed up in a whirl of color and then receded. Tom felt his stomach rise into his throat. The pilot swung the helicopter around in a wide arc.

"We'll find them, Tom," Jeff promised. "I swear we will." The agent sounded confident. But his expression was grim.

Jessica shielded her eyes against the snow glare. "We're catching up with him," she said in a tense voice, eyeing the black motorcycle that sped along the gully a few hundred yards ahead of the convertible. She couldn't decide whether the news was good or bad. "I still don't know what we're going to do when we catch him."

"The Grand Canyon must be up ahead somewhere," Elizabeth said. "I thought we'd have reached it by now. But I don't see any sign of it, and it's too big to miss. We must still be a few miles away."

"Just out of curiosity, Liz, why are you giving a geological tour while we're chasing a killer?" Jessica asked.

"Because once we corner him at the canyon, he won't have any choice but to stop and surrender to us."

Jessica sniffed. "Or to pick up his revolver and blow us away."

Elizabeth patted the canvas duffel bag, now on

the seat beside her. "He's not the only one who's armed," she reminded Jessica grimly.

Jessica stared at her in amazement. "Liz! I can't believe I'm hearing you talk this way. What happened to my pacifist, violence-never-solved-anything sister? You sound like Rambo."

"I'm not saying I want to shoot him. I'm hoping he'll give himself up when he sees that we've got the rest of his guns and ammunition."

"But he knows how to shoot! We don't! And his bike is working fine, but I'm starting to hear a weird rattling noise from this heap of Rick's."

"I don't hear anything," Elizabeth replied. "And as for Scott, we'll have the edge on him in every other way. Scott's on a bike, which gives him no cover, while we've got a car we can duck down in. He's got one gun. We have three! And his will have to be reloaded after six shots."

"But he wants to kill us a lot more than we want to kill him," Jessica pointed out. To her mind, that made up for any advantage the twins might have. She focused on Scott's jean-clad body up ahead. Revulsion, regret, and desire churned inside her. Fear overwhelmed them all. "Liz, what if we really have to shoot him? I can't do it! I know I can't!"

"I hope it doesn't come to that," Elizabeth said quietly. She stared straight ahead, her eyes thoughtful. "If we do have to kill him," she continued, "we're in much bigger trouble than we are

271

now. Scott's the only witness we've got who knows we didn't kill that clerk in Moapa—even if he's not willing to say so. If he dies, we'll get nailed for that. And for murdering Scott, too."

Jessica was barely listening to her sister. A noise had been hovering on the edge of her consciousness for several minutes. Now it grew undeniably loud. *Thwonk-thwonk-thwonk*. "Liz, what in the world is that noise?"

Elizabeth shrugged. Then she grasped wildly at the wheel to keep the car from swerving into the rocks along the edge of the gully. A black helicopter loomed over them, rising like a monstrous insect from behind the snow-dusted cliffs.

"Jessica!" Elizabeth's scream was weak against the clatter of the helicopter. Jessica whirled in her seat. A swarm of police cars appeared on the horizon, converging toward the green T-bird. The cars were still distant; their sirens were masked by the *thwonk-thwonk-thwonk* of the helicopter overhead. But their lights flashed like colored fire.

Jessica sank back into her seat and closed her eyes. "We're trapped," she whispered.

"They're too close to the rim!" Tom cried, pointing frantically out the side of the helicopter. The green convertible was racing toward the yawning chasm of the Grand Canyon. "The cliffs are in the way," Tom said. "They can't see the canyon from the ground!"

Jeff knew Tom was right. Scott's motorcycle was much more easily maneuverable than the twins' old Thunderbird. Scott was leading the Wakefields right to the edge of the canyon. Then he would probably veer out of the way as they plunged to their deaths.

Jeff's requested backup was on its way; a dozen police cars were converging on the site, looking like a swarm of ants from up in the helicopter. But the cars were still far in the distance. Scott had a wide head start on them all. He could easily hide in this expanse of wild land. Or he could have—if not for the two men who peered down at him from the helicopter.

But Jeff didn't care about Scott right now. Jessica Wakefield and her sister were his first priority. And they were in a car speeding straight toward a mile-deep canyon.

Jeff grabbed a megaphone. "Stop the car!" he called to Elizabeth, in a voice turned tinny by the device. "You're heading toward the edge of the canyon!"

Tom pounded a fist against the metal side of the helicopter. "They can't hear you!" he cried in frustration. "The chopper's too loud. They're going to go over!"

Jeff shook his head. "Not if I can help it," he growled. He leaned forward to give the pilot some instructions.

"What did you tell her to do?" Tom asked.

"There's no time to explain. It's risky, though, so hold on."

Jeff felt hope welling up inside him. *This really might work.* If nothing else, it was a plan. He'd felt so helpless through much of this case—it felt good to be *doing* something for a change. He knew that catching Summer's killer wouldn't bring his fiancée back. But rescuing Jessica Wakefield from the same man might help fill a small corner of the emptiness that had gnawed at him since Summer's death.

"What about Scott Culver?" Tom asked.

"He'll have to make his own choice. But I have a feeling he isn't going to like the options."

Elizabeth's mind was racing even faster than the convertible, which bumped and bucked through the creek bed. The black helicopter loomed overhead, following their every move. The gully was shallower now, Elizabeth noticed. The cliffs were reduced to low ledges, and the creek bed was littered with rocks.

Jessica was near hysteria. "Oh, God, Liz!" she kept screaming. "What are we going to do?"

"I don't know!" Elizabeth answered, shouting to be heard over the noise. "I can't even hear myself think. Are they saying something to us? I thought I heard a voice."

"How am I supposed to know? They're probably saying, 'Stop or we'll shoot!'"

Mercifully, the hovering helicopter lurched forward, toward Scott's bike. The *thwonk-thwonk-thwonk* subsided slightly, unmasking the thin whine of police sirens, still far behind.

"We have to keep going straight!" Elizabeth cried. "It's our only chance. We can still catch Scott if we corner him at the rim of the canyon. Maybe he'll give himself up—or even try to kill us."

Jessica stared at her. "Are you out of your mind? You sound as if you want him to!"

"I said try, not succeed." Elizabeth made an effort to sound brave for her sister's sake, but she was as terrified as Jessica looked. "If the police see Scott fire at us, maybe they'll realize that he's the criminal, not us."

"And maybe they'll think he's a hero, helping them catch the dangerous Wakefield Gang! If Scott doesn't kill us, the police will!"

"Calm down, Jessica. If you've got a better idea, just—"

"*Liz!*" Jessica screamed.

The helicopter was dropping to the ground, directly in front of the convertible. Elizabeth slammed on the brakes. The car whipped into a tailspin.

To Elizabeth, the next thirty seconds seemed to take an hour. Jessica cowered in her seat, hands blocking her face as if she could stop an impact. Elizabeth pulled on the steering wheel, fighting to control the car as it careened toward a low cliff that rose over the gully. Ahead, the helicopter glided to earth. Its metallic black form looked garishly ugly against the tan swells of the plateau.

Suddenly the cliff was rushing toward Elizabeth, as if it, and not the car, were racing forward. It grew into a massive stone wall that filled her vision with a terrifying hulk of red and tan rock. Then there was a sickening splintering noise as the convertible smashed into the cliff. Elizabeth screamed as the car's green hood folded like an accordion.

"Run!" Jessica yelled as soon as she realized that she and Elizabeth were both in one piece. Sitting in the car, unable to save herself, had been as nerve-racking an experience as Jessica could remember. Now at least she could *do* something. She pointed to another row of low cliffs. "Maybe we can lose them in those hills!" She grabbed Elizabeth's arm, yanked her from the car, and began to run.

Jessica dropped her sister's hand as she clambered over a large snow-topped outcropping of sandstone. "Hold on, Liz," she instructed. "It's slippery on top." She jumped to the ground on the other side and reached up for her sister's hand. Elizabeth hadn't begun to climb. Instead, she stood motionless, her blue-green eyes wide as she stared at the helicopter. Jessica followed her gaze. A slim, broad-shouldered young man stood beside the helicopter, his head down, under the force of the propellers. He gestured frantically, cupping his hands over his mouth as if he were yelling. But his voice was lost in the rattle of helicopter blades and the strengthening scream of sirens.

"Tom!" Elizabeth yelled. Then she raced toward the helicopter, as if all her problems were over.

Jessica knew better. As she watched Elizabeth collapse into Tom's arms, she noticed another figure emerge from the helicopter. It was a tall, well-built man in his mid-twenties, holding what looked like an assault rifle.

Fifty feet in front of the helicopter stood Scott, straddling the motorcycle. The afternoon sun glinted off the barrel of his revolver. The man near the helicopter was gesturing at him with the rifle. Jessica guessed that he was an FBI agent, but she didn't understand what was happening. She stared at Scott, with the wind tossing his light-brown hair, and she couldn't think at all. In a daze, she stumbled toward the two men.

Suddenly Jessica knew the truth. She rounded the helicopter, and the low cliffs that had blocked her view fell away. A sheer chasm opened in the rock plateau, a few feet beyond Scott. The Grand Canyon. Jessica stopped, feeling sick. Scott had been leading the twins over the edge of the yawning canyon.

Somewhere behind her back, the sirens were

much louder. She sensed cars skidding to a halt on the snowy plateau. She knew police officers must be jumping out of those cars, their guns cocked.

But the agent near the helicopter was clearly in control. In a flash, she knew that the agent was giving Scott a choice. The only way he could avoid capture was to plummet off the rim, into the depths of the canyon. Certainly the agent didn't mean for Scott to kill himself, Jessica thought. *He must assume Scott will turn himself in.* Scott stared back at the agent, unmoving. A line of tension seemed to stretch between the men, like a taut wire, holding their gazes on each other.

Then the line snapped. Even before Scott made a move, Jessica realized that he would never allow himself to be arrested. She closed her eyes, horrified. "No!" she whispered.

Scott gunned the engine. He turned to blow Jessica a kiss. Then the bike kicked up a fountain of dirt and snow. And Scott sped forward until he plunged over the rim and into the Grand Canyon. Seconds later a fireball roared up from the gorge, reflecting amber in the snow. Jessica staggered toward the edge of the canyon, tears blurring her vision.

Strong, comforting arms encircled her from behind. The FBI agent gently led her back toward the helicopter, where Elizabeth and Tom were holding each other as if they'd never let go. Jessica buried her face in the handsome agent's warm sweater, crying tears of relief.

"It's all over now," he murmured, holding her close. "You're safe." Something in the man's warm, brown eyes looked calm and at peace. And Jessica knew that he spoke the truth.

It's Your
First Love. . .
Yours *and* His.

Love Stories

Nobody Forgets
Their First Love!

Now there's a romance series
that gets to the heart of *everyone's* feelings about falling in
love. *Love Stories* reveals how
boys feel about being in love,
too! In every story, a boy and
girl experience the real-life ups
and downs of being a couple,
and share in the thrills, joys,
and sorrows of first love.

Coming soon

Here's an excerpt from
Love Stories No. 1,

My First Love

THE NIGHT THAT Rick Finnegan kissed me changed my life—but not in the way I'd expected.

He had given me a ride home from my best friend Blythe Carlson's house, where we'd all been drilling one another on vocabulary for the PSATs. There we were, sitting in his dad's Buick outside the Palms bungalow apartments, where my mom and I live, when, out of nowhere, Rick slipped his arm around me.

I don't know what got into him, but one minute he'd been defining the word *alacrity,* and the next thing I knew he was demonstrating it. He moved across the seat so fast that I didn't have time to react. Suddenly his gaping mouth was on mine. Instinctively, I closed my eyes—and he kissed me.

283

"Amy, I—I think I'm starting to like you," Rick whispered.

My eyes flew open in surprise. But instead of seeing Rick, I saw Chris Shepherd, who's on my swim team, the Dolphins, and who's in my physics class, too. He's also the guy I've been daydreaming about for weeks. "I'm the one you really want," Chris-in-my-mind said. I gasped and jumped away from Rick, leaving him to kiss air where my face had been.

"Rick!" I shrieked, staring at him.

"Amy?" Rick said, looking sheepish. "Are you mad? What's wrong?"

"N-n-nothing," I stuttered, trying to collect my thoughts. I couldn't believe that Rick Finnegan—Mr. Practical and my long time friend—had just kissed me!

I put my hand on his shoulder. "Look, Rick," I said gently. "I'm very flattered. You're a great guy. But we're friends—and I'd like to keep it that way. I don't have time for romance."

But Rick didn't look convinced. "Amy," he said, twisting a lock of my straight blond hair around his finger, "you know what they say about all work and no play. . . ."

"Maybe," I said, stepping out of the car, "but all play and no work gets you a career dipping cones at Dairy Queen."

Actually, I didn't say that. I didn't even think up this perfect comeback until the next day. What came out instead were my mother's words, words often meant for me.

"Your passion is misguided," I informed him, closing the car door behind me.

"My *what*?" I saw Rick's lips form the question behind the window glass right before I waved and turned away.

I couldn't believe I had said that. Mom uses *passion* in a totally different way, as in *enthusiasm for something*. It has nothing to do with feelings for someone. I felt kind of bad saying that, but I didn't know what else would work. Rick and I have known each other since elementary school, and the kiss really caught me off guard. I turned again to go back and apologize, but he was already driving away.

I stood for a minute outside our bungalow apartment, looking up at the stars and thinking about the fact that one of my oldest and best friends had just kissed me. When did Rick's feelings for me change, and why didn't I know about it? I had felt nothing when Rick's lips were on mine. But for some unknown reason, just the thought of Chris Shepherd's lips sent my heart racing. It was true, what I'd said to

Rick—I never *had* had time for guys. Until now.

Chris and I had known each other for a couple of years from the swim team, but he had never treated me any differently than any other girl on the team. He was always friendly, and he kidded around, but that was it.

I had always liked Chris, but over the last few months I had been noticing different things about him—admiring his long, lean body; his thick, glossy brown hair; his quick sense of humor . . .

I shook my head to get rid of the thoughts. I had feelings for Chris I'd never had for a guy, but I was still too shy to do anything about it. He had been a fantasy tonight and he'd probably always be a fantasy, I thought dejectedly as I headed inside our bungalow.

"You're just in time for the latest episode of *Search for the Stars*," Mom said as I walked into our combination living/dining room. Mom worked two jobs. She worked from nine to three at the Arizona Bank, and evenings at the El Rancho supermarket. Everyday she taped her favorite soaps, and in the evenings she'd curl up on the couch and watch them.

"Thanks, but I've been studying vocabulary for hours," I told her. "I'm afraid I'll erase what I've learned if I zone out on TV."

"Good for you," Mom said. "You go ahead and get a good night's sleep."

"I think I will." I hesitated for a moment. "Mom? Something pretty weird just happened," I said.

"What?"

"Well . . . Rick drove me home from Blythe's. And . . . he . . . well, he, um . . . told me he liked me," I explained, blushing. I didn't think I needed to tell her about the kiss. It was kind of embarrassing.

Mom sat up straight. "What did you say?"

"I told him I didn't like him that way. That we were just friends." I watched as Mom breathed an almost undetectable sigh of relief.

"Good answer, honey. With your schedule, a boyfriend is the last thing you need," she said.

"Yeah. I guess," I said, shrugging.

I kissed her on the cheek and went to my room. There's no way I could have sat through the soap. I was having a hard enough time putting Chris out of my mind and concentrating on my work. The last thing I needed at the moment was to fill my aching brain with stories about star-crossed lovers and abandoned dreams.

The PSAT, it turned out, was a nightmare of words I'd never used and math I'd understood for about an hour in ninth grade. It was bad enough that my brain was fried from choosing among *A, B,C,* or *none of the above,* and that my hand was numb from filling in those tiny circles with a sweat-slick number-two pencil. But the worst part was the reel-to-reel reruns of that kiss that played in my head all day.

And it wasn't Rick's kiss that I kept seeing—that was something we both wanted to forget, I was sure. It was Chris's. I couldn't stop picturing what it would be like to kiss him. In my mind his lips were soft and warm and firm. Then, when his lips found mine, I had that roller-coaster feeling—my heart plunged into my stomach and then began the slow, suspenseful crawl right back up to my chest.

The next thing I knew, I was sighing so loudly that people on both sides of me turned and stared. At the same time the proctor announced, "Fifteen minutes left." What was I *doing*? How could I blow this? Embarrassed and frantic, I raced through the rest of the test.

288

★   ★   ★

I was relieved when the PSATs were over, though considering my state of mind when I'd taken it, I was worried about my score. As we left the room, everyone seemed to be talking at once.

"Did you finish the analogy section?"

"How do you find the least common denominator in fractions?"

"Does anyone know what *apposite* means?"

For the rest of the day my honors classes were a chorus of collective anxiety. When my last class was over at three o'clock, I fled to the gym, where I hoped to somehow rinse myself of it all by putting on my racing suit and plunging into the pool before practice.

The rest of the team wasn't due to help put in the lanes for another half hour, so I had the open pool to myself. I love swimming more than anything else in the world. As I stood on the deck and looked at the tranquil water, I began to feel calm. For the next two hours, all I'd have to do would be concentrate on picking up another win in the 200 freestyle this weekend.

I took a few running steps and blasted the water's smooth surface with a cannonball. As always, the water was chilly, so I started swimming warm-ups, steaming back and forth from end to end. Believe me, after two seasons on the swim team, I knew that pool so well that I could swim it in my sleep.

By the fourth lap, I was cruising—when suddenly I crashed into someone and swallowed a mouthful of water.

"Amy, are you alright?" asked a soft male voice as I surfaced, coughing. It was Chris.

"I'm fine," I said, coughing again. I wiped the water dribbling from my mouth off my chin. "I didn't see you."

"I'm sorry," he said. "I saw you swimming laps when I got into the water. I should have gotten out of your way. I know it sounds stupid, but I was just floating on my back and thinking." He looked at me with real concern. "I'm sorry."

"Don't sweat it," I said shyly. "It's just that I thought I had the pool to myself." I wanted to duck my whole face underwater or at least hide my eyes. Could he tell by looking, I wondered, that my mind was spinning constant reruns about kissing him?

Chris returned to floating on his back. His brown hair fanned out like a paintbrush behind him. "If you close your eyes," he said, "you can pretend it's a lake, it's so calm and quiet."

I watched him as he lazily kicked his legs and drifted, eyes closed, toward the middle of the pool. "What are you doing?" I asked.

"I'm watching myself break the regional record for the breaststroke," he explained.

Great, I was thinking, *while I'm picturing kisses, he's imagining fame.* Nervously, I asked, "Do you really think imagining something can make it come true?"

Chris laughed. "I'll know when I reach the finish line."

Even though he looked sort of strange floating there, I admired his quiet determination. Chris is the fastest swimmer on the Dolphins, but breaking the breaststroke record was something that he had never been able to do.

I loved watching him. His body was long and thin, yet muscular. I'm about 5'7" and pretty thin myself, but I don't move as gracefully as Chris.

Several Dolphins came into the pool area then, their voices sending echoes across the floor tiles. Not even this commotion disturbed Chris's concentration. I wondered what part of the race he was mentally swimming just then.

As he drifted nearby, I wanted to reach down and gently stir the water, send it rippling to

291

touch him. Instead I ducked my head back under and continued swimming laps.

I swam freestyle for a few lengths, feeling confident in the water—until I made a graceless flip turn, whacking my heel against the lip of the pool.

"Ouch!" I yelled. I hadn't meant to cause a commotion, but as I limped along the side of the pool to the starting blocks, I could see that Chris was moving toward my lane. My heart skipped a beat when I realized he was waiting for me.

"Your timing's off," he told me when I stopped to get my breath. He touched my wrist, and I was suddenly aware of his long, strong fingers. I stiffened, and he must have noticed, because he took his hand away immediately and let it skim the surface of the pool.

"That's what Coach August says," I said, trying to sound casual, as though my wrist weren't burning from his touch. "He says I turn too late."

"Not too late, exactly, but too cautiously. Your turn would be right on target if you didn't mentally pull back just as you got to the wall. It's like you trip yourself up."

Chris was probably right—it wasn't so much the turn but the dread of it that kept me from swimming full speed. I constantly imagined bashing my heels. And that was exactly what kept happening.

"You could do a neater flip turn and probably shave twenty seconds off your time if you didn't hold back and just charged," Chris said. "Otherwise, it's like you're swimming with your mental brakes on."

"That makes sense," I said. "But how do I charge if I'm terrified I'll hit the lip of the pool?"

"By picturing doing it perfectly so many times that you really believe you can." He waded over to grab a kickboard from the pool deck. "First," he said, tossing me the Styrofoam board, "you've got to relax. Here, float and breathe deeply." He walked over and steadied the board.

But it was hard to relax with Chris staring down at me. I lay there looking up at him. All I could think about were his deep-set brown eyes. There was an intenseness in them, and a kindness as well. I felt like I was about to blush.

"Good so far," Chris said, gently brushing his fingers across my brow. "Now close your eyes."

I squeezed them shut and waited. "Not so

tightly," Chris advised. "What do you see?"

You, I wanted to say. Aloud I said, "I see myself lying on a kickboard, looking stupid, in the middle of the pool."

"Amy, be serious."

"I am." At first I was too self-conscious to imagine anything but the rest of the Dolphins making fun of me. But after a while I got the hang of it. I saw myself in the practice pool, speeding toward the end of the lane. I was surprised that the mental picture was so vivid. "I'm swimming," I said, still feeling kind of silly.

"And?"

"I'm watching the lane lines, getting close to the lip."

"Okay, now try to imagine keeping up your speed. What are you thinking?"

"Don't hit the lip, don't hit it, don't hit it—wham!" I opened my eyes then, and instinctively reached down to rub my heel.

"Try again," Chris said gently.

"What's the use?" I moaned. "I can't do it."

I thought then that he'd give up, but instead he urged me on. "This time, instead of thinking 'don't hit it,' try thinking 'flip.'"

I closed my eyes and was mentally halfway down the lane when I stopped midstroke to ask, "Why?"

"Because your brain takes the 'don't' out of 'don't hit the lip.' And your body only does what your brain tells it to."

If that was true, I was in trouble, because there were plenty of my mother's "don'ts" rattling around in my head. *Don't apologize for your intelligence, don't mope about what you don't have, don't take your education for granted, don't underestimate yourself, don't expect something for nothing, don't throw away your future on some guy.* For years I'd been repeating those commands in my head, maybe dooming myself to do the very things I'd told myself not to.

In my mind I began my stroke again, saying "flip, flip, flip" under my breath, swimming as fast as I could imagine. Then, before I knew it, I'd turned in the water almost effortlessly.

"Hey, I did it!" I said, and opened my eyes in time to see Chris looking at me intently, studying me the way I'd studied him.

Just then Coach August blew his whistle, signaling it was time to put the lanes in for practice. I slid off the kickboard and let myself sink. "Thanks," I said shyly.

"Anytime," Chris said, smiling. Then he turned away and swam toward the coach.

Anytime, I thought happily as I dove under-water.

Anytime . . .

I was the last one to leave the girls' locker room after practice that afternoon, mostly be-cause I was thinking so much about Chris that I couldn't get moving. As I walked out of school, he was sitting in the grass by my bus stop.

I was surprised. He lived on the east side of town, and I lived on the west. "Hey, Chris," I called out as I crossed the street. "Aren't you waiting for the wrong bus?"

"I was waiting for you," he said.

I thought my heart would stop. "Me?" I managed to say.

He smiled as he stood up and brushed the grass off his faded, torn Levi's. "Yeah," he said. "I thought you might want a ride home."

"You've got a car?"

He pointed in the direction of the school park-ing lot behind me. "It's my brother Dave's. It's that sixty-four Mustang," he said. "Dave said I could use it today. He's home on break from college."

I turned and saw this gleaming classic car. I knew that Chris came from a pretty wealthy family, but because he always wore Levi's with holes in the knees, T-shirts, and baseball caps, I

296

had never thought about it. "Cool," I said as we walked toward the convertible, trying to conceal the excitement I felt.

Chris opened the car door, and I got in. As he slipped into the driver's side, I glanced at him out of the corner of my eye. Just the night before, I had been in Rick's car, being kissed by him and seeing Chris. Now I was actually in a car with Chris! Maybe thinking about things really could make them happen.

We hope you enjoyed reading this book. If you would like to receive further information about available titles in the Bantam series, just write to the following address, with your name and address:

Kim Prior,
Bantam Books,
61–63 Uxbridge Road,
Ealing,
London W5 5SA.

If you live in Australia or New Zealand and would like more information about the series, please write to:

Sally Porter
Transworld Publishers
(Australia) Pty Ltd
15–25 Helles Avenue
Moorebank
NSW 2170
AUSTRALIA

Kiri Martin
Transworld Publishers (NZ) Ltd
3 William Pickering Drive
Albany
Auckland
NEW ZEALAND